REBECCA HIRSCH GARCIA

THE GIRL

WHO

CRIED

DIAMONDS

& other stories

Published by ECW Press
665 Gerrard Street East
Toronto, Ontario, Canada M4M 1Y2
416-694-3348 / info@ecwpress.com

Editor for the Press: Jen R. Albert
Copy editor: Crissy Calhoun
Cover design: Caroline Suzuki
Front cover photograph: © Nora Hutton (@norahutton)

LIBRARY AND ARCHIVES CANADA CATALOGUING IN PUBLICATION

Title: The girl who cried diamonds & other stories / Rebecca Hirsch Garcia.

Other titles: Girl who cried diamonds and other stories

Names: Garcia, Rebecca Hirsch, author.

Identifiers: Canadiana (print) 20230466915 | Canadiana (ebook) 20230466923

ISBN 978-1-77041-727-4 (softcover)
ISBN 978-1-77852-203-1 (ePub)
ISBN 978-1-77852-204-8 (PDF)
ISBN 978-1-77852-205-5 (Kindle)

Subjects: LCGFT: Short stories.

Classification: LCC PS8613.A715 G57 2023 | DDC C813/.6—dc23

This book is funded in part by the Government of Canada. *Ce livre est financé en partie par le gouvernement du Canada.* We acknowledge the support of the Canada Council for the Arts. *Nous remercions le Conseil des arts du Canada de son soutien.* We acknowledge the funding support of the Ontario Arts Council (OAC), an agency of the Government of Ontario. We also acknowledge the support of the Government of Ontario through the Ontario Book Publishing Tax Credit, and through Ontario Creates. We gratefully acknowledge the financial support of the City of Ottawa.

PRINTED AND BOUND IN CANADA

PRINTING: MARQUIS   5   4   3   2   1

For Tanya.
I promised I would try.

A GOLDEN LIGHT

AFTER HER FATHER DIED Sadie stopped moving.

It started with her throat. The day her mother called and told her he was dead she opened her mouth to scream or cry or shout or something, and nothing came out. She pushed her throat muscles together and moved her tongue around until she felt ridiculous and then, at last, a bubble of sound slowly pushed its way out of her mouth. It was a tiny, tinny *no* quickly buried underneath the sobs which flagged in and out from the receiver. She tried again to say something more, but this time she spoke only silence.

Hello? her mother called over the receiver. Sadie, hello?

I will never be able to talk again, Sadie thought mournfully, and she placed the phone back in its cradle.

But the loss of sound was only the beginning. It was soon followed by a loss of movement. Walking up or down a flight of stairs became an insurmountable effort; soon even walking on the flattest of flat sidewalks seemed an undertaking too painful to bear. She began to feel as if she was struggling underwater each time she stood up on her own two feet. By the time of the funeral her hands had become slow and dim-witted, clumsy and uneasy to manoeuvre.

At the burial Sadie stood in the front row, and as they lowered the casket into the ground, she realized that she could no longer hear the morbid sounds of the coffin scratching along the dirt. She strained her head forward, listening for the sounds of sobs and the indelicate noise of noses being blown, but there was nothing except a strange humming void.

I've misplaced my ears, she thought, and tried to remember if she had put them on that morning or had simply gone out without them.

She looked around for her sister or her mother or her brother-in-law; instead she caught the wandering eye of a middle-aged woman, some variant of cousin or family friend. She touched Sadie's hand, her eyes watering in a fresh wave of tears. Be strong, Sadie read off the woman's lips. Sadie nodded vaguely and let her hand be clutched, let herself be dragged into the sea of black cloth that wept and reminisced on her shoulder. They all seemed so sad, but Sadie, dazed from the loss of her senses, kept forgetting what they were being sad for.

After the burial she fell under a wave of exhaustion. She couldn't make it to the car; on the way out of the cemetery she sat down to rest on a little bench marked Viner and never got up. If it wasn't for her brother-in-law, who noticed her absence in the car and came looking for her, she might have remained there forever, hunched on the bench like a small frightened creature. He found her sitting there, her fingers roaming desperately over her ears, as if to reassure herself she had not lost them. He had known Sadie since she was a little girl and when he saw her sitting there, looking for her lost ears, it was as if they had fallen through time and were children again. He plucked her up from the bench and carried her to the car where her mother and sister were waiting. She fell asleep before he had finished buckling her seat belt.

The next thing she knew she was back in her parents' house, surrounded by people she did not know who all seemed to know her. Her mother did not know what to do with her, so she was ensconced among the nearly dead, a group of forgotten wheezing elderly people who pinched her cheeks roughly with their papery fingers and patted their leaking eyes with wrinkled handkerchiefs. Sadie could tell from the force of their expirations on her skin that they were shouting their words into each other's dim ears. She was grateful that she could no longer hear them and slid her eyes away to avoid reading their lips. And then, as she waited, hearing nothing and feeling nothing except the slow, mournful reverberations of many feet on the living room floor, she felt her limbs petrifying. Her eyelids began falling slowly down, then up, then back down again. Terrified, she somehow managed to excuse herself and stumbled away towards the stairs. She crawled up the steps to the warmth of her old bed, kicking off her shoes and curling, blissful-deep, under the covers. When she woke it was dark outside and the warm, familiar body of her sister was curled cat-like around her.

Get out, she said, or tried to say. She found she could still turn over and so she did that and wedged her elbow cruelly into her sister's side, wriggling deeper and deeper until she woke up. What? her sister queried in the raspy voice of the newly awoken, but Sadie was deaf to her.

In a quick minute the last of Sadie's patience was lost, run off perhaps to join all the sounds which she could no longer hear or make. Rallying the last of her strength she planted her feet firmly into her sister's back and pushed her off the bed.

She could feel the slam of the door that indicated her sister had left. When she could not sense even a trace of angry feet stomping down the hallway she began to regret having pushed her out. She felt very small and alone in the dark of her room and for a while there was no difference between her opened eyes and her shut ones. She thought she had gone blind. She wanted to go and hug her sister and beg her forgiveness for her own selfishness and say, I'm sorry I can't cry with you, I'm sorry I can't give you what you need, I love you, but it was already too late for that. She had grown roots, she was immobile, and her vocal cords had died away, so rather than try to uproot herself she fell asleep instead.

When she woke up again her mother was there. It was morning and she was smoking and staring out the window, smoking as if nothing had happened, as if she belonged there in Sadie's room by her window, as if Sadie were a little girl again and her mother had come in to check on her daughter, the most natural thing in the world to check on your daughter, leaving her husband alone in their bedroom to sleep. Sadie tried to think of the last time that they had been together in this room and she fell upon a memory of long ago. When she was little she had lost her sister's hat and her sister had yelled at her and her father was gone, as usual. It had been her mother who had coaxed her into opening the locked door of her room, who had pulled her onto her lap and told her that there was no use crying over spilt milk or lost hats and kissed her until all the tears ran away.

She willed her mother to come to her again as she had come to her before and run her hands through her hair and hold her as she cried. Instead she stood there smoking as if she hadn't realized that Sadie had woken up and that she needed her. She was filled suddenly with an insensible hatred, a pulse of anger which coursed through her body making her flush with fatigue. Get out, she started to say and fell asleep halfway through saying it.

The psychiatrist that her mother lured up to Sadie's room told her that this was normal. She wore a beautiful plum skirt suit and round-toed brown shoes, the same shoes that Sadie owned, the same shoes she had worn to the funeral and then kicked off her feet on her way to bed. Sadie thought their matching shoes were a sign, from God, the universe, or whoever, and so she stared at the shoes as the psychiatrist told her that there was no normal reaction to grief which, conversely, meant that any reaction was normal. As she said this, Sadie realized that she could hear again. The suddenness of this abrupt return of sound and sense startled her; she almost began to laugh. Instead the laugh turned into a yawn which went on for a century in which everything stayed exactly as it was. The psychiatrist blinked and the yawn was broken, the century over in a second. The psychiatrist asked Sadie all sorts of questions which Sadie might have answered had she been able to speak. I need to sleep, Sadie thought as her eyes closed and she drifted off. The psychiatrist seemed to understand.

Sadie's mother and sister and brother-in-law all took turns watching over Sadie. Our Sleeping Beauty, they called her as they watched the slow rise and fall of her breath. They humoured her for a few weeks. A sleeping girl, after all, requires nothing but a little food and a little worry, and the worry was a blessing, a reason to look in front of themselves and not into their own hearts. They prodded her gently into wakefulness and tried to feed her the lightest of foods: juice and Jell-O, dried toast and soup. She nibbled at their offerings in a daze then fell into sleep again and again. They tried to get her to talk or to move or to see, but it seemed she could no longer do any of these things very well at all. They brought in doctors who sometimes said her soul was sick, or that she was a medical mystery, or that there was nothing wrong with her at all. The latter type of doctor they considered to be complete quacks and they would be sure to always smile and nod, being kinder and gentler than they would have with someone they considered sane. No matter the doctors' opinions of Sadie, no one knew how to fix her. Her family began to believe she was broken forever and adjusted themselves accordingly.

And then a strange thing happened. Sadie woke up one evening to find her room lit up in gold. It was the magic hour, the last hour of sunlight of the day, when everything was bathed in golden light and the warmth of the fading sun made the colours of the sky glow ember-bright. She wondered if she had read that in a book or if her father had told her that. And as she thought that word, the word *father*, a golden flicker burst into the golden room and danced across her legs and arms and face before settling gently on the wall beside her bed. She reached out and placed her hand upon the dancing flicker. Papa? she asked.

It was the first word she had spoken in a year.

In the morning she was a little better. She sat up in bed and said please and thank you to her mother's shock and amazement. For a few minutes strung together she had a brief, quotidian conversation about breakfast foods with her sister. But her mind was elsewhere; she could think of nothing but the flicker of light, a beam of brightness in a field of gold.

From then on, every evening at the magic hour, the golden flicker danced into Sadie's bedroom. She placed her hands on the light and let it thread through her fingers. She found that the flicker let her fall asleep with her heart at ease and wake up in the morning with the strength to last through the day. She could get up and get dressed and go downstairs and eat breakfast with her mother like a normal person. She could hear and speak and move her limbs, her flesh no longer cold as a statue. She could be good for her mother and strong for her sister, she could count on both hands over and over again the good things that she did every day. Yes, she was good. One morning they ran out of milk at breakfast and she volunteered to go to the corner store and buy more. When the cashier flirted with her she flirted back and gave him the first smile she had been able to give since before her mother had called her that long, long time ago. She was happy, in a way.

One night she went to her room at the hour only to find her sister already there. She was sitting on Sadie's bed with a book in her hands and when she heard Sadie's footsteps she looked up at her with a smile that reached out to Sadie's heart. She opened her mouth to speak only to close it again and Sadie wondered wildly if her former disease was catching and her sister had gone mute as she once had.

The sun was setting and the room had turned a brilliant gold.

Look, her sister said.

It was the magic hour and the flicker danced in a beam of light between them. Sadie's sister reached out her hand and Sadie's light, a glimmer of brilliance in a room of gold, played across her fingers. Suddenly Sadie felt happy: happy that her sister was in her room and that she had seen the light and that Sadie could explain everything to her. She felt sure quite suddenly that her sister would understand, that she was the only one who *could* understand, and that even if Sadie hadn't stumbled upon her sister in her room unexpectedly like this, she would have brought her here eventually in order to show her the flicker. Sadie reached out for her hand and saw that she wasn't looking at the flicker at all anymore, but out, out through the window. She turned to see what her sister was looking at and saw her little next-door neighbour, a child named Tanya, whose room was directly across from her own. She was playing with a pocket mirror, flicking it lazily back and forth, now catching the light, now letting it go. It flashed across Sadie's face and for a blissful second she was blind.

DAMAGE CONTROL

IN THE MONTHS BETWEEN 11th and 12th grade, at the behest of absolutely no one, Leonard Lawrence lost weight. A lot of it. Sixty-nine pounds to be exact, enough to just about make up one ten-year-old boy or maybe two four-year-old ones. If you stuck to averages. Which Leonard did.

Leonard looked it up on his computer, was constantly looking up weird weight-related things on his computer that summer when he ate next to nothing at all and half of him disappeared in a snap like a vanishing trick. The next to nothing that sustained him, when he binged, usually at night to avoid the questioning stares from his parents, was mostly ice cream (plain chocolate preferably) and room-temperature Coke (the ones that came in cans with the tabs he could twist back and forth and then snap off). Sometimes, for variety, he would throw a bag of salted potato chips into the mixture. He would sit there in the dark of his room, lit by the flicker of his computer, choking down the nauseatingly delicious mixture until there was nothing left and then he would stack the cartons and cans in a neat pyramid at the back of his closet and carefully fold and pleat the empty chip bags into his sock drawer. Sometimes in his weight-related internet prowling he would stumble across material which detailed the symptoms of eating disorders and Leonard would skim them, allowing the faint feeling of recognition to flutter across his mind for one unsettling second even as he was reaching with his mouse to X out of the tab. No one in Leonard's family, not his parents or his younger sister, Leah, or even really Leonard himself, thought of what he was doing in those terms. Eating disorders were what happened to wealthy white girls with ribs you could count when they lifted up their shirts. Eating disorders were what overbearing mothers passed down to their daughters, a legacy of cutting women down to size until they disappeared completely. Leonard was a half-Black, half-Jewish boy with a wide teardrop-shaped nose and a hulking teardrop-shaped body. His father called him husky, and even as he had slid from fat into obese, his stomach spreading outwards like the universe, his mother could only be coaxed into admitting he was just a little zaftig.

No, what Leonard was doing was simply losing weight.

He showed up the first day of 12th grade expecting to be seen. This was what a lifetime of being a loner who watched movies instead of having friends had taught him. Whip off your glasses and run a hand through your hair and bam! you're Ally Sheedy in *The Breakfast Club* or Rachael Leigh Cook in *She's All That* or motherfucking Superman in every Superman comic, TV series, or movie ever. So losing those 69 pounds (that elusive 70th pound just temptingly out of reach) in Leonard's mind made him the equivalent of a god. He was sure that this year not only would everyone notice him and find him wildly clever, charming, and sophisticated, but Karen V., she of the blond hair and the creamy skin and the bouquet of girlfriends who followed her everywhere, would literally genuflect at his new Adonis physique and blow him at her house. Or in her car. Or behind the bleachers. (Leonard had a lot of fantasies.)

Instead what happened was that maybe two people did a double take when they realized who he was and then those people clumped off into groups and talked about what everyone else was talking about, which was Margot Ordona. Margot Ordona who, depending on who you talked to, had tried to kill herself, fallen out a window, or been run over by a car sometime in late July. She had disappeared abruptly last summer. One day she and Karen V. were supposed to go to the movies and Margot just never showed. A day later she received a call from Margot's mother that Margot was in hospital. No further details forthcoming.

That was the story from Karen V. who was holding high court in the art hallway, her navy-blue eyes wet with tears.

She won't see anyone, Leonard heard her say as he fiddled with the lock on his locker, pretending not to eavesdrop.

I mean, like, I'm her best friend and she won't even talk to me.

The bouquet bobbed and nodded around her and Karen V. sniffled and opened her wet mouth in a way that made parts of Leonard twitch and the bouquet leaned their heads forward in eager anticipation of what else she was about to say. The hallway fell silent, and people stopped breathing and even the janky fluorescent hall lights stopped flickering and held themselves steady, everyone waiting for Karen V. to speak. And then the bell rang and she giggled and said, Oh shit, I'm gonna be late for homeroom, and that was the last Leonard heard about Margot Ordona till she came to school the next day sporting a lightning-shaped scar across her face.

People who heard the news second-hand shrugged.

Well, that wasn't so bad was it? A little lightning-shaped scar was something a girl could pull off, something a girl could be disproportionately ashamed of, in the way girls often were about Monroesque beauty marks above their mouths and heart-shaped birthmarks on their thighs, pretending like these were disfigurements and not something that made them more adorable in every way.

Only this wasn't some cutesy Harry Potter type thing. More than one person actually shrieked when they saw Margot, and Leonard, who by the time he caught sight of her in second period had been warned, still had to bite down hard on his lip to keep from sucking in a sharp gasp of air. No, the scar on Margot Ordona's face was physically distressing to look at. It began at her brow and paused at her left eye before continuing down over her cheek in a ripple before it hooked delicately just under her jawline, taking up a David-Bowie-in-his-Ziggy-Stardust-era length of real estate on her face like a tribute done in scar tissue. Whatever stitches had once held her face back together were gone, but the scar was still painfully raw as if it might just split open again. It was all anyone could see when they looked at her: first carved flesh and then the remnants of Margot Ordona somewhere beneath that, like a double exposure.

She had cut off all her hair too. It was what Leonard found himself fixating on, partly because staring at the scar was uncouth and partly because it was the only thing he really remembered about Margot Ordona pre-scar: the black swaths of her hair that fell midway down her back like an inky river. Karen V. used to play with it during lunch, braiding it into thick ropes with her milky hands, her skilled fingers working with a feverish dexterity that made Leonard wish that they were at work on him.

There were rumours that Margot Ordona had hacked it all off herself the night before school, and Leonard could just imagine the quiet zig-zig of the scissors as they worked, all that beautiful thick hair falling away in awkward, jagged clumps. That was why, the rumours went, she had come to school a day later than everyone else. Her mother had freaked and called around and hired someone to come to the house and even out the strands like Margot Ordona was a rock star whose service people came to *her* and not the other way around like the average pleb. Her mother insisted on bangs, people said, to try to hide some of that raw scar tissue, but it didn't end up mattering anyway since Margot pinned it all back with bobby pins. Allegedly (and this really must have been a rumour because Leonard couldn't imagine how anyone would know) Mrs. Ordona had walked into the room and gasped out a single breathless Why? of horror upon seeing her daughter, and Margot Ordona had laughed and said, The better for you to see me, my dear, and snapped her jaws click-clack like a wolf.

Leonard didn't know why anyone would do that. He didn't know why Margot Ordona in particular would do that, because the Margot he remembered was timid as a Victorian-era virgin, her hands constantly fluttering in her lap and her sour mouth turned down. She had always looked unhappy and this, Leonard supposed, was because she had always been second best, first loser, the one who no one saw behind the dazzling white light of Karen V.

Leonard had learned from TV that this did something weird to girls: that it addled their minds and made them familiar with the tickle of their fingertips deep in their throats and the slice of Bic razor blades skating across the street of their wrists. Or, in Margot Ordona's case, made her a sulky sweet that no one could bear to swallow down.

Only the Margot Ordona who came back after that summer, with a broken face and an eyebrow that drooped under the bulk of scar tissue, was no longer the passive little consumable that watched, unblinking, as boyfriends and friends turned their faithless eyes to Karen V. The Margot Ordona who came back was hungry and wanting and all bite.

Leonard never would have believed it possible, the way he would never have believed he could lose 69 pounds and be ignored, but people got used to Margot Ordona's scar. By November, they weren't talking about it at all even though it was still a bright enough red to match the dying autumn leaves. What they were talking about instead was how Margot had made all six of her fall semester teachers cry. She had told Mrs. Zhao, going through a divorce, that she would die alone. She had told Mr. McAvoy that he was a pathetic pedo who got off on failing ninth graders. She was the reason the police visited the school twice, both times because she was found smoking a blunt in plain sight in the music hallway. In the middle of English class (and this was something Leonard actually witnessed, slouching in his chair and feeling his soul depart his body as it happened) she stood up and said she refused to partner with Jake Riley in *Death of a Salesman* scenes because he was a nasty little rapist-in-training who liked to stick his hands up the back of girls' shirts and snap their bra bands.

After the Jake incident Leonard, along with about seven other socially delayed mouth-breathers, lurked outside the admin offices where Margot Ordona was being questioned. They were like a pack of acne-riddled vultures, desperate to know what was going to happen. He heard and saw next to nothing, but his position did allow him to get his first and only glimpse of Margot Ordona's mother, a pocket-sized white woman with blond hair who succeeded in making her daughter look Hulk-like beside her. Leonard heard her before he saw her, the sharp double click of her heels against the cheap linoleum of the school floor authoritative and comforting. She was fiddling on her phone on the way in and still fiddling with it when she came out five minutes later with Margot Ordona trailing behind her.

I swear to God, I'm going to sue the entire fucking school, Mrs. Ordona said as she walked off. She turned the corner and then came back when she realized that Margot wasn't following her, lifting her head from her phone for the first time. Her eyes were a surreal blue, like ice. It was terrifying.

Margot, she said and actually snapped her fingers, as if her daughter was a dog.

Come on.

Margot shook her head. Her back was to Leonard and the rest of the boys (only boys) who had been waiting for a glimpse of her as if she were a queen and not a delinquent. Leonard had no idea if she knew they were there; he, along with the seven others, pretended they were considering the candy in the vending machines.

I can still make the end of fourth period, Margot said.

Her mother blinked at her once.

We should have sent you to private school, she said. Fine, go to fourth period. Try not to make anyone else cry.

The motherly advice dispensed, Mrs. Ordona left and Margot turned around and headed in the direction of her groupies who were now frantically scrambling away, some peeling down the hallway, darting into the guidance office, and one idiot spinning round and round in circles, flinging his hands about. Leonard, who stuck by the vending machines, feeding change into one of them, was embarrassed to be associated with him even if only by virtue of being in the same hallway.

If Margot was aware that she was the cause of the meltdowns she gave no indication. She continued steadily on her path, but she stopped just in front of the vending machines where Leonard hadn't punched in any numbers. He pretended to consider his choices as he stared at Margot's reflection in the cheap glass. Her reflection made her scar look like a distortion, a flaw in the glass and not a part of her face. She was close now, very close, but she gently reached past him and punched in D3, making Leonard's choice for him.

You're welcome, she said as she left.

D3 was a kind of joke, black licorice that no one ever bought and had been in the vending machine since before Leonard was born probably. As far as Leonard knew he was now the only person to have ever wasted pocket change buying it. A fair punishment, he guessed, for staring at Margot when he had no business doing so.

Leonard ran to class where even as he was apologizing for his absence he was, in his head, talking to Margot Ordona, telling her he appreciated her joke and that she looked like her mother, even if her mother was a tiny middle-aged white woman and Margot was a teenager with distinctly Asian eyes (epicanthic folds, he learned they were called later that night after pausing his internet wanderings from calculating and recalculating his BMI. Or plica palpebronasalis, which he disliked because it sounded like a disease). He wanted to tell Margot that he'd thought about it and it was their chins that made them look alike. The same points that curved just slightly to the right. That and the way they held themselves, like royalty. He wanted to ask her how she did that, how she could look right past everyone like they didn't exist even while everyone was staring at her.

Instead of having his Coke and ice cream brew, that night he chewed his way through the tough black licorice, his jaw aching.

Leonard found he had a lot of things he wanted to talk over with Margot Ordona. The more he talked them over in his head, the more he thought of new things to ask her to the point that conversations with her began to rival his sexual fantasies involving Karen V.

He thought that maybe he could be friends with this new, torn Margot Ordona. That maybe if she saw him and they could talk, just a little bit, she wouldn't try to make him cry.

It happened between classes. Before Leonard knew what was what he was falling down and smashing his chin along the gritty tiled floor of the music hallway. In his zest to escape the swing of the auditorium door as it rushed towards him he had whirled away with such effort that he tripped over himself and crash-landed on the floor. Leonard rolled over trying to spot the source of his humiliation only to find himself in the bizarre position of looking up Margot Ordona's skirt. As blood hit the edge of his tongue and heat pooled in his cheeks he turned his head delicately away to avoid seeing something he wasn't supposed to.

If Margot knew that at that angle she had exposed herself she gave no indication. She didn't seem ashamed at all as she kneeled down beside him and tilted his chin up with one surprisingly strong finger, the nail digging sharply into his under-chin which was sore from where he had bashed it. He didn't want to look her in the face, didn't know what it would be like to see all that twisted-up scar tissue just inches from him, but he felt the pads of her fingers reaching out to soothe where the nail had stung and the touch of her hand was so soft that he found his eyes flicking upwards involuntarily.

Her tongue darted out and licked her top lip right on the cupid's bow and that's what he was looking at when she said it.

Hey you, she said. Didn't you used to be fat?

Leonard had never, not once, not ever, been in trouble before. He was the type of student who, in elementary school, had gotten called into the principal's office to claim attendance and behaviour awards. In the administration office waiting to be told off, his face throbbing and the total shame of what he had done closing up his throat and threatening to drown him, he found himself looking to Margot for comfort. Margot who was slouched in her seat as if she were in her living room while he sweated uncomfortably in the pool of his too large clothes, the ones he had refused to toss even after he lost all the weight.

He had never wanted to hit a girl before and he still didn't but when Margot Ordona had asked him if he used to be fat something in him had snapped. That she was the only one who had noticed and that she had brought attention to it filled him with an anger he couldn't explain, even to himself. Which was the only excuse he could come up with for what he had said.

What did you say you Harvey Dent–faced bitch?

The music hallway had gone silent. Half the hallway (the nerdier, distinctly male half) had gasped dramatically. The other half, which included Margot Ordona and Karen V., just looked confused. Margot Ordona's brows drew together, her face a mess of confusion that made the scar tissue pucker.

Leonard had wanted to die both because what he had said was so cruel and because it was the worst, the most pathetic kind of insult, one so ineffective that it needed an explanation to work. He opened his mouth to clarify, at least, that it was an insult. Before he got a word out a fist came out of nowhere.

Somewhere from far away, while rolling around on the floor, sobbing with an abandon that reminded him of the primal furies of toddlerdom, Leonard was conscious of a teacher demanding explanations. Even though he was sure his face had been broken open as wide and as deep as Margot's there was enough in him to be able to hear Margot claiming responsibility even though it was a boy (the name Tiernan Josh appeared to him) who had given him the kiss with the fist. So Margot and Leonard had both been hauled off to the principal's office, no one brave enough to act the snitch.

By the time they arrived and were told to wait Leonard felt more ashamed than anything. Even though his cheek was tender to the touch, the pain was receding quickly. His own tears and fear that his face was broken now seemed like a disproportionate response to so small an event. The teacher who had brought them in had unearthed an ice pack and a compact and Leonard had been allowed to examine his face, which had only just begun to swell and showed no traces yet of a bruise.

Margot, innocent for once of the crime she was accused of, lost interest in Leonard and pulled her phone out of her skirt pocket and started scrolling through it.

When she found what she wanted she nudged Leonard and tilted her phone screen at him.

She had pulled up photos of Harvey Dent, half his face eclipsed in burns.

This is what you think? I have a scar not a burn, Lard Lad.

Leonard felt the heat rise in him again, but this time he had the pain in his face to chasten him and he turned away.

In the end they were set loose with a series of warnings that amounted to hot air. Principal Wilson made the key mistake of inter-rogating them at the same time and Leonard, feeling guilty, claimed that he had hit his face himself when he tripped.

Why did you say it was your fault? Principal Wilson asked Margot.

Margot shrugged.

He tripped over my feet. That teacher didn't even ask questions, just assumed I was guilty.

Principal Wilson looked helplessly at Leonard, and Leonard tried to pull off a Margot-like shrug of nonchalance and ended up wincing from pain instead.

Margot was set free but Leonard had to wait for his mother to take off from work and come pick him up.

On the way home from school he asked if they could stop for a treat, and since he had been so good with his diet, and for so long, Leonard's mother bought him a box of drugstore chocolate chip cookies. He turned down dinner to lock himself in his room and ate the chalky cookies one after another, chewing through the pain, until the entire box was empty.

Somehow, even though they had been the only two people in the principal's office, word about Margot Ordona calling him Lard Lad got out. Leonard certainly didn't speak of it and he didn't imagine that Margot was in a great huff to tell anyone either, but she must have. Must've let it slip to Karen V. one day, must have squinted her eyes and screwed up her fucked-up mouth in a way that wrinkled her fucked-up face and asked what that former fat kid's name was, because suddenly people were coming up to Leonard and doing exaggerated double takes and saying, Hey, Lard Lad, didn't you used to be fat?

The weirdest part was that no one was trying to be mean. They were actually trying to be friendly. Friendly because the new, legendary Margot Ordona had baptized him with her bitchiness the day she noticed him in the hallway.

Even Tiernan came up to him and clapped him on the back in a kind of apology.

We cool, LL? Tiernan had said and Leonard, scared of a second punch, simply nodded.

Leonard didn't know what to do with it, with this new ability to be seen. It wasn't funny for him and it became a whole lot less funny as the months wore on and Leonard went from being a former fatty to a current one. He blamed Margot Ordona for that.

Because ever since she had exited the principal's office he found himself thinking about Margot Ordona and eating everything. The Coke cans weren't stacked neatly anymore, and the ice cream cartons had taken over the closet.

Karen V. was reading Lady Macbeth in English and when she said, *What, will these hands ne'er be clean?* in her flutey voice Leonard thought of himself at night with his fingers stained with potato chip grease, or whipped cream, or jam. He would lick his fingers clean, promising himself that this time would be the last time. Only it never was and by the time spring rolled around he was halfway back to his heaviest weight and wholly back to being invisible.

Maybe not as invisible as he would have liked to be. In class Karen V. clapped her hands to get everyone's attention when the teacher stepped out of the room. Leonard focused on her right away (he still felt that uncontrollable tug that made him aware of her whenever she stepped in or out of a room) but everyone else took a moment to settle. No one had much patience for Karen V. She still commanded a certain respect, but only in so much as she was the one who was closest to Margot Ordona, Margot who continued to fascinate with her reckless cruelty.

Everyone, Karen V. called out, clapping her hands once more until enough people were finally looking. If she cared about her plummeting stock she didn't show it. She smiled widely, friendly as ever, and invited everyone to a surprise party for Margot.

Leonard stopped listening after that. He knew that everyone did not actually include him so he was surprised when, after the bell rang and class broke up, Karen V. caught up to him as he barrelled down the hallway, her long legs easily matching his get-the-hell-out strides.

Hey, she said as she tapped him on the shoulder, nearly causing him to trip. Leonard briefly wondered what it would have been like if Karen V. had been the one standing over him that day. Different, certainly. Karen V. always wore jeans.

Hey, you should definitely come to Margot's party. She smiled and he looked down, unable to meet her eyes. He was embarrassed by how badly he wanted her to like him, still.

Oh, he started to come up with an excuse, but Karen V. was already holding out her hand for his phone and Leonard found himself handing it over, waiting awkwardly as she tapped in her details.

I know Margot wants you to be there.

She touched his shoulder and squeezed it lightly and then left, jogging through the hallway on her way to her next class.

Margot Ordona lived in an apartment downtown which, to Leonard, meant that she was poor. Everyone he knew lived in two-storey houses in the suburbs on winding lanes that curlicued into each other and sported names that sounded like granola bars. Nature Trail. Blue Willow. Thistlebrook Crescent.

It took Leonard two buses to get all the way downtown and another five minutes and a consultation with the sweaty crumpled-up sheet of paper with Google Maps instructions on it which he had printed out for safety since his data plan was shit. By the time he arrived in the lobby, stuttering an unsure thanks to the doorman, confused as to whether he was supposed to acknowledge him or not, he realized that Margot Ordona was the opposite of poor.

When the elevator doors opened on the penthouse apartment and a wave of happy drunken noises hit him, he had a sick feeling in his stomach. Margot Ordona was pretty fucking rich.

The first thing he saw were the bodies, clumped together in twos and threes, hands where they shouldn't be, at least not in public.

Leonard felt a flush creep over him, over the entire length of his bulky body, and he had never wanted more to be thin again so that there would be less of him to be ashamed.

He had to look away, he couldn't look away, he *had* to and then he must have because suddenly there was a whirl of blond.

Larry! You came!

It was Karen V. She gave him a sloppy hug and then whirled away from him.

Leonard, Leonard corrected.

Okay, Karen V. said smiling blankly.

It's the Lard dude, Tiernan said, coming out of nowhere, and then he was surrounded by a surge of faces he barely recognized, all cheering on the Lard Lad, a nickname that had stuck even as the irony of it had slipped away.

It wasn't a good time. Leonard drifted to the kitchen and then the dining room, circled back round to the living room where he hovered at the edges of every conversation. A girl he vaguely recognized as a 10th grader seemed friendly enough. She nodded at his inquiries for liquor and opened her mouth as if to answer before delicately bowing down and vomiting in a little pool that partially splashed on Leonard's shoes.

Leonard decided to find a bathroom he could hide in for a moment. There was a second floor to the apartment, one that everyone else seemed to avoid by consensus, but the first-floor bathrooms were occupied and Leonard felt the problem with his shoes was a pressing matter. When he ascended the stairs he was greeted with silence and rows and rows of doors. He hesitated, not knowing which one was the bathroom, not wanting to stumble in on anyone's private moment. Then he saw a door that was already open and went to it, vigorously pushing it shut behind him, closing out the noise from downstairs.

Margot Ordona was sitting at a vanity and brushing her hair slowly. She had grown her hair out a bit since the beginning of the school year and it now hovered at the tips of her earlobes. As she brushed she kept going past the ends and hitting her shoulders as if she were combing out the hair that she didn't have. The hair from before.

Hey, Lard Lad, she said when she saw him. There was something a little bit off about her, something that made Leonard sick to his stomach even though he was already sick to his stomach.

Someone threw up and it got on my shoes.

Oh, gross. Her nose wrinkled up. There's a bathroom through there.

Leonard followed her pointing finger to the bathroom where he took off his shoes and realized that nothing in his life and nothing in the bathroom, a series of pretty pinks and soft creams like something out of a Barbie Dreamhouse, had prepared him on how to clean vomit off his shoes. He blotted at them with a tissue and some hand soap that smelled like synthetic peaches, but all he succeeded in doing was rubbing the sick into the weave of his sneakers where, he had a feeling, it would never come out. As he rubbed he realized what had been so strange about Margot Ordona sitting all alone at her vanity brushing her hair. All of her scars were gone.

It's makeup, she said when he finally came out in his socks. He had left his shoes to dry in the tub, hoping to avoid putting them back on for as long as possible, hoping that when he returned for them they would somehow be clean.

She raised her hands as if she were going to touch her face and then dropped them again as if she couldn't bear it.

My mom wants me to get plastic surgery. Apparently there's shit they can do with lasers. It's . . . whatever.

That's great, Leonard said.

Margot squinted at him and as she did her scars puckered, just a little, so that you could see them if you knew where to look, which Leonard did.

Take off your shirt, Margot told him, which was when Leonard's brain began short-circuiting. For all of his dirty shameful thoughts about Karen V. he had never even held hands with a girl outside of forced activities like eighth-grade square dancing. Kissing was something he would have liked to do someday soon but it hadn't happened yet. He was suddenly very conscious of the way his heart beating kept the blood flowing in his body and he felt sure this meant that he was going to have a heart attack before Margot Ordona could finish having sex with him.

Oh my God, you little pervert, Margot said, her eyes scanning his face and reading his panicked thoughts.

I'm not going to fuck you. Just take off your shirt.

The relief was so great that he found his fingers obediently tugging his T-shirt over his head before he had really thought about what he was doing.

He had only looked at himself once in the mirror since he had lost all the weight, standing naked in front of the full-length mirror in his bedroom. He still had dreams about it. Dreams where he looked in the mirror like he had that day, only in his dreams his skin was smooth and perfect and he couldn't stop touching it. As if she knew about those dreams Margot made him stand in front of the mirror after she had told him he was ugly, made him look at what he had done to himself, the stretch marks as fresh and as raw as Margot's scar. Like a cat had clawed at his stomach. At his hips. His shoulders. Symmetrical rips that would never leave his body. When she flicked his stomach the loose skin rippled in a way that seemed less like flesh and more like a pool of water. He hated himself so much he wanted to cry.

Lard Lad, she said. She was so tender when she spoke, her voice gentle and quiet, just right for the two of them alone in the room.

You're disgusting. You're beyond ugly. You're repulsive.

For some reason the words didn't sound so bad in her mouth.

Now do me, Margot said.

What?

Margot had a little blue bottle of something and she poured some of it on a white cotton pad and began rubbing it on her face in broad strokes, wiping the makeup off so that the pad turned a tawny orange and the scars were unearthed, red from all the rubbing.

Do me, Margot kept repeating as she took up another pad and kept scrubbing.

For a second Leonard thought they were back to the sex thing and he hesitantly reached for the least sexual exposed part of her, her elbow, and was rewarded with a sharp slap to the offending hand.

My *face*, you idiot, Margot Ordona said. Do what I did to you.

You want me to tell you you're ugly?

Not like that. She shook her head a little impatiently. Tell me the truth. Please just tell me how ugly I am. Tell me I'm unlovable. Just tell me.

Leonard looked at Margot's face. Up close he could tell she was drunk. She looked so hopeful, so earnest, her face rid of tension and smoothed out. Still, her brow bone drooped a little. The scar ruined the purity of her jawline where it tilted over her chin. The truth was people would look at Margot Ordona for the rest of her life and they would see the scars and they would wince and then they would get over it. She was no beauty but Margot Ordona was no monster either. Even with her face full of makeup, the scars buried in plain sight, and even the year before, when her face had been untouched and Margot hadn't even known that that was something she should be grateful for, and even now with a magnificent scar, Margot was alright.

Up close, overpowering the alcohol, she smelled like perfume, something musty and expensive that turned his head. Up close the outlines of her scars gleamed in the light.

Leonard wanted to touch them, but what he wanted more was to live.

Well? she said.

You're okay, he said.

It was quite something to watch her face fall. For a second he thought she was going to punch him the way Tiernan had, but instead she just picked up his T-shirt and threw it at his head, where it settled as gentle as a cloud.

You suck, Leonard Lawrence, Margot Ordona said. It was a bit weird to realize she knew his full name. He tugged his T-shirt back on and she went to the washroom to retrieve his reeking shoes.

He spent the rest of the weekend binge-eating and thinking about all the ways that Margot would punish him. He dreaded Monday, thought about pretending to be sick, but he was still working out the details of how he would go about doing that even as he entered the school lobby.

Then the first bell rang and it was too late to really do anything but slouch to class.

At lunch he walked down the music hallway and saw Margot and Karen V. eating alone in front of their lockers.

Karen V. was flicking Margot's hair and Margot was laughing.

Leonard walked by. He kept thinking that *now* she would say something, slowed his steps as he walked away waiting for it to happen. Only when he got to the end of the hallway and turned the corner did he realize that the moment wasn't coming. Because he had a soupçon of shame left Leonard did a long slow loop all around the first floor pretending for his own benefit he had somewhere to be, before he looped back around to the music hallway again. They were still there. He was still figuring out a way to call Margot ugly without getting kicked in the balls by Karen V. when he was almost past them.

Hey, Lard Lad, Margot said. She nodded at him with her chin, like a boy.

Leonard nodded back.

Hey, Harvey Dent, Leonard said.

And that was that.

MY FULL CATASTROPHE

GOING HOME WAS WHAT I was doing, going as fast as I could in an attempt to out-walk the cold. Already I could feel the needle-sharp cut of fall piercing my clothes, but I wasn't going to take a cab or an Uber and let go of any of my hard-earned dollars, not that night after my new headphones had broken right before I started my shift and I was walking in Converse that were sporting a week-old hole at the heel. I could have taken the bus I suppose, but waiting for the bus at night can be a dangerous thing; like everyone in Ottawa, I know one or two people who have seen someone stabbed at Rideau Centre.

So I kept walking as fast as I could, just another tired girl on her way home after a long day spent mostly on her feet. I had only one mission: get home and into bed. I wasn't thinking of anything else. And then I did the stupidest thing possible: I cut through the pedestrian underpass.

Everyone knows not to walk through the pedestrian underpass, especially not alone, especially not at night, especially if you're a girl.

Everyone I know has sworn to their mother, father, sisters, brothers, girlfriends, boyfriends, friends, or whomever, that they will never do something as stupid as walk through the pedestrian underpass alone at night. And everyone I know, especially if they are a girl, has broken this promise more times than I can count.

I didn't want to do it, not that night or any other, no one ever wants to do it, but the reasoning went a little something like this: it is cold and the quickest way to get from where I am at the corner of Rideau is to cross the street and go through the underpass, instead of crossing the street, waiting for the light to change, crossing the street again, and then walking way out of my way up Wellington, where I will have to wait to cross two more times at the tricky little crosswalk.

But con: the underpass is scary.

But pro: you will get home faster.

But con: there might be someone lurking under there, the strange man with the hammer who has been stalking downtown Ottawa, or some unknown rapist, or some hobo, moaning for change or grunting harmlessly in his sleep who will make you scream when his shuffling reaches your hyper-alert ears.

But pro: you will get home faster.

But con—

But I didn't care about the cons anymore. The light had changed and my feet had made the decision for me. As I neared the underpass I hunched over in a defensive position, steeling myself for whatever the dark, urine-soaked tunnel might offer me. In my ultra-terrified state the shadows seemed like passable imitations of human life forms and I forced myself not to scream as they flickered close by me. It was all a lot of nothing, was what I tried to tell myself, but I should have skipped the soothing speeches and paid closer attention to where I was going. In a second I had tripped and fallen and scrambled away on hands and knees, my palms scraping against the disturbingly slimy pavement. I was out of the underpass and at the top of the steps, the adrenaline rushing through my body before I realized that the thing I had tripped over had cried out when I stumbled on it. I shuddered at the memory of hard flesh pressing against my hand. Shivering at the top of the steps, I waited for the thing to come lurching out from the shadows so I could run headlong into the street, cars be damned, and burst through the doors of the Château Laurier screaming until they called the police.

I waited and waited and waited and no one came out.

The longer I waited, the more I doubted what had happened. Was there someone down there? Had I mistaken rotting fruit for a warm hand? I went back down the steps a little and called out, hoping to hear a response, hoping to not.

Hello? I said. Hello?

My voice echoed back, reed thin.

Go, I told myself. Go home. Go now.

I waited.

Help me, came the voice. Please.

It took me a moment to blink back my terror and realize that this was a real true dyed-in-blue emergency. Still, I hesitated a moment before dialling 911.

I realized much later that no one would have blamed me if I had waited for the police at the top of the stairs, though how much that would have changed things I couldn't really say. In any case I shouldn't have gone back down there no matter how much he called for me. It was the 911 operator with her stupid voice urging me on, making me want to be a better, braver person that made me go down there and check.

What's your name? she had asked me.

I could hear the tapping of computer keys over the line, a gentle reassurance that this woman was doing something for me.

Leora, I said.

Listen to me, Leora, are you sure someone's hurt?

I don't know.

Leora, she said. Leora?

She kept saying my name over and over again from somewhere far away and safe and warm and well-lit. I knew that that was probably a trick that they taught her when they trained her to answer emergency phone calls. Repeating someone's name was reassuring, it established confidence, kept them in the moment. I knew all this but I couldn't help it. I was reassured anyway.

I'm going to go see, I said.

I'm right here, Leora, she said. Which was a lie.

Two minutes later I was crying, and not with compassion. I was scared and cold and hungry and all I could think was please God, please, please don't let him die in front of me, let him die after, I don't care, just don't let him die in front of me, I've had too much shit happen, I can't take anymore, I can't see it, I can't.

I kept shifting away from the puddle of vomit that occupied the brief space between my legs and his head.

You're going to be okay, I said, trying to wriggle my fingers a little to see if his grip would loosen. It did not.

My nose was beginning to run so I wiped it on the sleeve of my coat, my free hand still clutching my cellphone. The light from the screen illuminated him in sickly neon; if it hadn't been for his hand crushing my fingers between his own I could easily have mistaken him for a discarded mannequin.

Medics are coming soon, I should go check, I said as I shifted onto my knees, preparing to get up.

No, he said, his hand still gripping my hand, eyes locked on my eyes. It was so dark, even with the thin window of light from my phone, that I couldn't tell what colour they were. They seemed to be wholly black, like a demon's.

If I'm going to die, I'm going to die with you by my side. I've done a lot of bad things in my life, he said, but even so I know God wouldn't let me die alone.

You're not going to die, I said.

I tried to keep my eyes focused on his black ones, tried to speak in a calm and even tone, but everything about me was beginning to clatter and shake: from the cold, from the fear, from the exhaustion of keeping my body as tense as it was. I trembled like a possessed marionette, the disjointed movements seeming to come from elsewhere.

Tell you what, he said.

I felt a fleck of foam land on my hand and shuddered, twisted my whole body in an involuntary reflex; still I couldn't cut free.

I'll make a deal with you. You let me live and I'll never touch the stuff again. You understand?

I didn't though. I didn't understand anything except that I would have given everything I had to be anywhere but there. I wished him dead a thousand times over. In a minute I would be clawing at him myself, urging him towards the grave, if he did not let me go. He pulled me close. His mouth smelled like a dead thing.

Yes, I said, nodding. You're going to live.

Our hands together were a mix of cold sweat and grit.

Wasn't it important to keep him talking or to talk to him, or something? I had wasted years of my life watching TV shows with situations exactly like this and I couldn't remember a damn thing.

My name is Leora, I said.

He nodded like that was the best thing he had ever heard.

I work in the mall here, at the restaurant just there.

Just there, he repeated.

I babbled on, facts of life, the only things I could remember at that moment, my name and birthdate and the names and birthdates of everyone in my family, the time in second grade when the class had been divided into suns and moons for God knows what purpose and I had been a sun and sprinkled glitter in my hair and had found the stuff buried in my scalp for weeks and weeks after, and how the cold had been burning through my jeans to my kneecaps and now I could feel neither the burning nor the cold.

Did you hear that? I kept asking him, and when he nodded back I made him repeat back a little of what I had just said.

The EMTs found us like that, eyes and hands locked together, when they came running down into the underpass, their emergency flashlights crudely lighting the two of us.

Six months later I walked into my kitchen and found him making an omelette.

He looked different in that he looked like a regular guy, the ones you see walking down the street every day and pay no attention to, except maybe a little more wiry than most. It was the fact that he looked so ordinary, and didn't smell at all like urine, that completely threw me off, and for a moment when he turned and smiled at me I thought that maybe my roommate had a new boyfriend. And then he waved the spatula at me and the sight of his hand wrapped around the handle made me remember.

Morning, Leora, he said. Do you know what that means, Leora?

Yes, I said, because I did.

It means my light, he said, ignoring me.

Know what my name means? he asked eagerly.

I wondered how he thought I could. When we had met it hadn't even occurred to me that he might have a name let alone that I should ask him what it might be and what it meant.

No, I said, because it seemed I had to say something.

But apparently I didn't, because he had already turned away from me and was opening up cupboards and searching for a plate.

I wished that this was a nightmare, but I knew that it wasn't. I wondered how he had gotten in and if he was going to kill me. I tried to remember what you were supposed to do in a situation like this, when a crazy person was standing in your kitchen making an omelette pretending like the whole thing was normal. I wanted to Google it, but my phone was past the kitchen in the living room and anyway I wasn't sure if Google, as infallible as it had always been, would have an answer for this one.

He pulled a chair away from the table and gestured at it like I was supposed to sit there. I plunked down in the one furthest away, which was only a couple of feet from the chair he had picked for me.

How did you get in here? I asked halfway through the omelette. It was good, but as I licked cheese off my back molars I wondered if he had poisoned it.

Your roommate let me in, he said. He gave a weird little laugh and I tried to smile back at him as if this was all normal.

Evidently I was a terrible liar because that was when he came closer to me, asking me what the matter was.

I think you should go, I blurted out. I had a vague idea that I should try to keep him calm, try not to anger the strange man standing in my kitchen where there were plenty of knives around, but I couldn't help myself. It was as if an itch had invaded my whole body and it wouldn't go away until he went away, until I was alone in my apartment again.

Get out, I said. Get out or I'll call the cops.

It had sounded like a plausible threat when I thought of it, but when I said it out loud it sounded tired and insincere like the dull way I asked Soup or salad? to my last customers of the night.

He gave me a crooked little smile, but he stopped moving towards me.

Hey, he said. Calm down. It's cool.

He raised his hands, palms up, and that was what really put me on edge. The fact that he was acting like *I* was crazy when it was my apartment. My kitchen. I picked up the only weapon within reach, the knife I had been using to cut up my omelette. A string of cheese drooped down its tip like a mangled flag. I don't think I could have really done anything with it, but the weight of it felt good in my hand, and I knew that if I had to I could draw blood.

Okay, he said. Cool. Okay.

He backed out of the kitchen. When he got to the living room he called out to me, See you 'round, Leora.

I tried to put the rest of the omelette in the garbage and do the dishes, but my hands were shaking on their own. Eventually, after dropping a cup on my toe and watching it shatter everywhere, I gave up and sat down in the living room, staring at myself reflected in the dark screen of the TV, waiting for my hands to be ready to listen to me again.

They were back to normal by the time my roommate came home. By that time, I thought maybe it would be better not to mention it at all. I did though, feeling that surely this was something you were supposed to communicate to your friend and roommate, if only to ask them to be more vigilant before letting strangers into the house. It was strange though; in the retelling it became something different from what it had actually been, something a little funny and weird.

After I finished telling her what had happened we sat in silence, unsure of what to do.

Well, she said after a while, maybe we should call the police?

I shook my head.

Nothing really happened, I said.

She floated the idea of calling the police a few more times throughout the week, but eventually she too came to regard the whole thing as a non-event. It wouldn't happen again, we told each other. The guy was some ex-druggy who was just a little too eager to thank me for saving his life. It was a fluke, like winning the lottery or finding a five-dollar bill on the ground, except it was bad.

Only one morning, when I had almost forgotten about the whole thing, I saw him standing across the street from my building when I left for work. When he saw me he gave a hesitant wave. I ignored him and walked as fast as I could towards the bus stop, boarding the first bus that came, the wrong one of course. In my confusion it took me three stops to find my bus pass, the driver growing more and more impatient with my fumbling the whole time.

The police wouldn't do anything. Or couldn't. The officer I spoke to, a polite man, confirmed that they would swoop in and arrest him the second he started hacking off my limbs with a knife but not a second before. He did, however, generously offer to have a talk with him and tell him to stop following me around. I looked down at this man in his neat polyester uniform decorated with shiny, toy-like emblems of authority. He was a good four inches shorter than me. If I sat on his chest I could crush him. I told him I wasn't sure that was going to cut it. They stopped taking me seriously after that.

He had started following me to and from work most days, so I began to take the bus instead of walking. I hoped that the flux of people would prevent him from stabbing me or, failing that, would at least be able to identify him as my murderer to the police.

It's a funny thing, but after a while I just stopped being so afraid of him. It was as if all the work it took to remain afraid, the locked jaw, the tensed shoulders, the constant awareness, were too exhausting to maintain.

I grew accustomed to his presence. It helped that for the most part the rides to work were uneventful; I would take my seat next to the window and lean my forehead against the dirty glass and he would take the one beside me. All he expected me to do was sit there as he talked on and on, a babble I was not required to engage with or even to listen to. He remembered much of the drivel I had spouted that night to keep his attention on me, and I was often reminded of this when he mentioned certain people or places or things that were important to me and were now apparently important to him too. And though we sat side by side he was careful never to lean in my direction or stray so much as a finger onto my side.

Since he had gotten rid of the smell that had clouded him when we first met it seemed no burden to have him there beside me. I had certainly sat beside stranger people and he was not really a stranger after all, there existing a sort of intimacy between us. Those few minutes in which he had clutched at my hand while I talked to him had apparently bonded us together in some unretractable way.

On good days I was able to think of it as some grotesque fairy tale in which he owed me a life debt. At night I imagined him pushing me out of the way of a car or rescuing me from a burning building, giving me a final nod before disappearing into the sunset, his debt repaid. In some ways, I thought of him as a puppy, loyal and needy and always there. Sometimes, in private with my roommate, I joked that he was my pet.

He usually got off the bus with me at Rideau and on my way from the station to the restaurant where I worked he kept close by my side, for he was usually accosted by a dozen or more people in the handful of steps it took to walk from the terminal to my work, mostly unwashed street kids in skinny jeans, lounging casually on pavement layered with gum remnants and cigarette butts.

Hey buddy, they would call out, all too familiar with his face, his slouch, that certain ropey thinness that spoke of untold energy, you looking to buy?

He kept his eyes straight ahead pretending not to notice them, but his cheek twitched at their words and he always breathed a sigh of relief when we hit the main doors and he could hold the door open for me, ushering us both inside.

I always wondered how they knew to sell to him; when I was alone I could forget that they were even there, step over and around them or just walk by. Without him I might as well have been invisible to them. One look at me and they understood I wasn't a user. When I was with him, they came alive. I was constantly in danger of tripping over their extended arms which stretched forward, reaching for what they could not have.

A man with no hands reached towards us once and I shuddered and jumped back. I knew you weren't supposed to admit that you were revolted, but I couldn't help it, the shiny stumps made me want to scream.

It was one of those things I couldn't stop thinking about, and he could tell because when we were far enough away from the man with no hands that he wouldn't hear us talking about him, he started to tell me about how sometimes people who had a part of them missing could still feel it even though it wasn't there.

Phantom pain? I said. Yeah, I've heard of that.

He reached out a hand tentatively to pat my shoulder and then thought better of it and pulled away.

Thanks, I told him later.

For what? he asked, and I found I had no answer.

I don't like coming downtown, he said to me once when we were a few blocks away from our stop.

Why not? I asked.

Too many memories, he said. And that was all.

But after that he started talking about how beautiful the rest of the city was and expressing his disappointment that I never seemed to venture further away from downtown than the Glebe.

What I like about you, he told me one late night when I was too exhausted by the end of my shift to do anything but let him speak, is that you're good.

I rolled my eyes.

You don't even know how good you are.

His hands were open, palms up, searching for words to express this goodness.

You're perfect. Pure, he said, not looking at me.

I think about it what must be like, you know, to be you, to walk around and not know about all the bad stuff that happens. It must be kind of wonderful, in a way, to be you and not know about all that stuff that goes on downtown. I'm a bad man, he continued. I've done things I'm ashamed of to girls who didn't deserve it.

The bus jolted and he leaned into me briefly, his arm brushing against my breast, before I elbowed him back where he belonged. He was trying to shock me I could tell, but I was unwilling to be shocked.

I turned my head away and tried to think about anything other than what he was talking about. I thought about a time when I was in high school and living in Westboro. My parents were holding a dinner party to which I was cordially not invited, they were always holding dinner parties to which I was cordially not invited. My father's friend had come upstairs to use the bathroom. I was supposed to be in my bedroom doing my homework, but I wasn't, I was going to my parents' room to watch TV on their big screen and we ended up colliding in the hallway.

Hey, he had said and then he pushed me gently up against the wall and slid both his hands from my shoulders to my breasts and I stood there not moving as he pressed himself against me and leaned down and kissed me and the beer that was on his breath was on me now and I felt sick because I knew what was going to happen next and it did happen, just not there and just not then because we heard a cough and he turned and looked around and my father was there.

Bathroom's that way, my father said and then he asked me if I had done my homework yet and I told him no and he said better get cracking, kid, and I went back to my room and didn't do it and the next day Mrs. Clarkson told me there was no excuse for not applying myself properly. I wondered if my father's friend had ever said that to someone: I took advantage of a young girl who probably didn't deserve it. I doubted he even thought about it that much.

The bus jolted me again and this time he pressed his hand onto my thigh to steady himself. He was still talking about how pure I was. I ignored the hand and told myself it was an accident, it was the jolting of the bus, and stared out the window and saw a homeless man and thought about all the homeless people I passed on my way to and from my apartment every day, how I didn't care if they were living or dead as long as I didn't have to cough up any change as I passed them. I wondered why I had to help the one man who didn't consider my having helped him a fair exchange for leaving me the hell alone for the rest of my life. I closed my eyes and swore I would never help anyone else again ever for as long as I lived.

Hey, he said. He moved his hand from my thigh to my arm and tugged.

It's our stop.

So it was.

It came to a point where I could ask him not to be there and he would listen. Don't show up when my parents are here. Don't be there the weekend my sister visits. Too many days of this and he would show up anyway, a quick walk by my window, a morning spent on my steps waiting for me to come down.

I couldn't hide him from all my friends though, and he soon became a fixture in our lives. I had to constantly remind my roommate not to let him wait for me inside our apartment no matter how cold it got outside. Still he found ways of being near me, walking behind us when we went to the store, and once holding my roommate's purse when she stopped to tie her shoelace.

Don't do that, I snapped.

Her hand hovered in the air trying to decide whether to hand over her purse or not. In the end she left it in his waiting hands.

He's not really dangerous, is he? she reasoned.

It wasn't long before she began to treat him like he was just another guy. I hated it when she talked to him. When I was out with her, or any other friend, I preferred to have him walk a few paces behind so I could forget he existed. She asked him what he did for a living and how he spent his days and why he was so obsessed with me and why he had been passed out in the underpass anyway and if he had ever been to prison and, when she found out he had, why. (Shut up, I told her, irritated beyond belief. Just forget about him.) She did shut up that time, but she never ceased to slip in a question or three when she thought I wasn't paying attention.

Have you ever seen anyone die, like, in front of you? my roommate asked him once.

He shrugged and looked away.

Is that a yes?

Yeah.

My roommate smiled at him in disbelief and he gave a shy grin back, a grin that grew each second she continued to look at him.

Let's go, I said as I tugged on her sleeve.

I didn't want her asking any more questions. It had occurred to me that maybe he had seen someone die because he was the one doing the killing.

But he would not stop talking, would not stop telling me what a bad and dangerous man he once was. He was careful to never give exact dates or names or times and as hard as I tried to Google my way to him, I could never find details about what he had done.

It was a terrible thing, he said the first time he told me, staring down at his knees, too ashamed to look me in the eye.

The whole thing was an accident, he said later on as we sat in the food court on my lunch break.

She deserved it, he volunteered one day, long after I had stopped asking him questions.

I did not ask him what she had deserved. I did not want to know.

The problem with not asking questions about his life was that he had more time to worry over mine. He never was comfortable with me working downtown, he never gave up on the idea that happiness existed if only we could go somewhere else.

You should get a job in Orléans, he suggested.

I shook my head.

Come on. There's plenty of places down there that—

I cut him off.

I don't want to work in the middle of fucking nowhere. If I have to work a crap minimum-wage job I'd rather work one close to home.

He shook his head as if I was being unreasonable.

But Leora—

Just fucking quit it, I said, much louder than I had intended to.

We were at the bus stop waiting and people were staring. A woman wearing a hijab gave me a look of disgust before wheeling her baby stroller off in the opposite direction. A man wearing dress pants and a blue shirt came over. His government ID dangled from his hip.

Are you okay? the government guy asked me. He bothering you?

Before I could say anything he had placed himself between me and the government guy.

We know each other, he said. It's fine, man, back off.

The man gave a little glance to me. He must have found something like confirmation in my face, because he turned and left, though not before giving an insolent shrug in my direction as if to say I had not been worth his time and he was sorry he had bothered.

Come on, I said and started to walk away, too embarrassed to keep waiting at that stop for the bus to come.

Can you believe the nerve of that guy?

He did the right thing. You could have been anyone.

It took him awhile to notice that I was not beside him, and when he did, he turned around and waited patiently for me to catch up.

As a compromise I quit my job and found another one in Chinatown. It was hard at first to be the new girl, the other servers at the restaurant treating me with indifference. Still, I liked working in a place that gave me free bubble tea and where no one knew anything about me.

What I really loved, though, was that he didn't like it. Where I saw Mary Janes and Hello Kitty and paper parasols he saw prostitutes and needles and all his old friends, the ones you could smell from half a block away, the ones who wore their grime like armour.

Get another job, he would say as the bus inched down Somerset. This is worse than your old one.

You want to put food on my table? Pay my rent? Just say yes and I'll walk right in there and quit, I'll do it.

Yes, he said, yes. But we both knew it didn't mean anything.

In Chinatown my new manager had little patience for him. My first week he followed me inside and drank endless cups of tea and gave tiny tips, little piles of dimes and nickels that were more of a nuisance than anything. At the beginning of my second week there I was warned about his presence. I protested loudly that he wasn't my responsibility, my cheeks flushing, and my manager believed me and took the liberty of banning him from the restaurant. I couldn't stop smiling, at the clouds, at the parking meters, at a passing man who at first looked confused and then tipped his head at me in acknowledgement and smiled back.

What're we gonna do? he asked me.

You can wait outside if you want, I said shrugging. I don't know about you, but I've got to work.

The city owned the sidewalk and so there was nothing my managers could do when he took to lounging around outside. Sometimes when I had a spare moment I would look out the restaurant windows and try to find him down below. He was always standing there waiting for me, reminding me of the sad-eyed dogs that were tethered to bicycle racks while their owners took their time browsing inside grocery stores.

Usually he was surrounded by a group of vagrants who orbited around him like flies. Though they never stopped coming to talk to him, they feared him and with good reason. He could sit there for hours listening to their recollections or taunts until suddenly he snapped and began yelling, upsetting their shopping carts, tossing their possessions like trash into the wind.

Whenever this happened my manager would be on the phone with the cops, complaining in an increasingly hostile manner that she was sick of all the goddamn hobos hanging around in front of the restaurant and could they please do something so that a good tax-paying woman could do her job in peace, *please*.

Once in a while the police did come. They didn't do much, just stood there with their hands on their hips trying to act authoritative and above it all as the winos pushed to see how far they could go without getting arrested. The hostile ones called the police pigs and chucked trash at their heads when they weren't looking. The friendlier ones would offer the officers a swig of whatever they had on hand and would complain in distorted voices about the world entire. None of them seemed the least bit afraid of being arrested. There was, of course, one person who was afraid of just that, but he was always gone before the police had pulled up to the curb.

How does he always know when they're coming? my manager asked once in exasperation, and I shrugged.

The summer came and I picked up extra-long shifts. The long days emboldened me and I gave up on the bus and took to walking everywhere, even all the way to work with him chasing me, whining in my ear, begging me to quit, begging me to give up on Chinatown. He had grown a beard, God knows why, the heat was enough to drive anyone mad. As we walked deeper into the heart of Chinatown a crowd gathered behind us, bored high-school-aged runaways and the old winos wheeling their wheezy shopping carts. I felt like I was at the head of a parade I did not want to be in.

Wait for me, Leora, he said.

Leora, the parade echoed behind him like a demented chorus.

It was embarrassing. I didn't want them knowing my name. I walked faster. He put his hand on my arm and shoved me up against the brick wall of a restaurant. His arms on either side of me, like a cage. It felt strange to be this close, to have his sour breath on my face. I couldn't hold his gaze and looked down, resenting him for making me appear weak.

When I say wait you wait, understand?

I nodded.

We stayed that way for what seemed like a long time. Long enough for most of the crowd around us to lose interest and wander away in the direction of the beer store.

One person stayed behind. A man or woman, I couldn't tell, swaddled in rags.

Hey man, they rasped, in a voice that sounded like someone had tossed their vocal box on the floor and then stepped on it, leaving it half-squished like a carton of juice.

Leave the lady alone.

He raised his hand as if to hit them and they scattered, dragging their rattling shopping cart behind them.

Come on, he said, you're going to be late to work.

It wasn't until I was counting my tips for the night that I realized we had walked the rest of the way hand in hand.

Look, I said, wait here. I'm just going to be five minutes, okay?

He had been in a nasty mood for days now. Twice in the last week he had made me late for work, adjusting the time zone on my phone and then by hiding my shoes.

Five minutes, I repeated. I just have to tell them I want to quit.

He looked as if he wanted to say something, but he swallowed the words and nodded instead. When I went inside the air conditioning flicked a shiver up my spine. I pulled my hair up in a ponytail and went to work.

At about noon there was the sound of yelling, of flesh hitting flesh, by the door. I paused in the middle of passing an order of rice. The whole restaurant paused. The noises got louder. I heard my name being called. The manager dashed into the hallway and stared down the stairwell, then ran back up and headed straight for the phone affixed to the wall behind the bar.

It's that weird guy downstairs who used to like you, she said, dialling by heart the number for the Ottawa city police.

He's done it this time, he's really done it this time.

We heard the sounds of glass breaking.

Another waitress went and peered down the stairwell.

Oh my God, she said when she got back, he broke the downstairs window.

We could hear more noise coming from downstairs. All the patrons had stopped eating, all the waiters had stopped serving. We stood in heavy silence listening.

It was strange, but standing there waiting I was reminded of when I was a little kid and I had to take all those tests and exams which were supposed to show how much you understood about whatever. I was never very good at those because halfway through I would just get bored and lay my head down on my arm at an angle so I could watch the clock, watch the seconds tick by. Only on those old school clocks the seconds didn't tick, the hand just went round smoothly over and over and over again in a way that was ridiculous in its simplicity. Like, of course the seconds were going to keep rolling forward, adding up the minutes that added up the hours that added up the days. And of course I knew the answers to certain questions on the test, just like I didn't know the answers to other questions. I didn't know why I had to write it all down when I could have easily pointed to each one and said, Yes, this I know. This I don't.

And standing there with everyone waiting for the situation to play itself out was just like that. I knew how this part was going to end.

After a while I couldn't take it anymore. I went to the kitchen, empty now, and poured myself a glass of bubble tea. By the time I had eaten all of the boba at the bottom it was like time had fast-forwarded past the parts I had anticipated. He was gone.

When my shift ended it was still light outside. I walked out the front doors, which had been covered over with cardboard and ignored the rust-coloured stains on the pavement outside. I walked home slowly, swinging my purse on my wrist. It was strange to walk like that, just me, down the street. I kept turning my head to look for the eyes that were supposed to be watching me and more than once I saw that I had snared the blank glaze of a no one. When they realized that I had caught them they shifted their eyes and their legs, crossed their arms over their chests, went back to fiddling with their phones or their rings or whatever and forgot all about me. And why shouldn't they? I was nothing to them. I walked on.

I wondered how long they could keep him in there. Probably not long. I wondered how angry he would be when he got out and if he would try to punish me for it. Let him try.

When I got home I left the door unlocked, opened the curtains wide.

THE COLDEST PLACE ON EARTH

YOUR SISTER HELENA THINKS that you and Alice should go on a trip.
Your sister Helena is 10 years older than you and has never gotten over
the fact that you are a married man now and entitled to make your
own decisions. Your sister Helena calls you morning, noon, and night
before you finally give in at 11:31 Sunday evening and tell her you will
suggest to Alice the possibility that perhaps you should consider going
on a trip.

Maybe.

It'll be great, Helena says. Just what you need.

You are not so sure.

You are talking about Andrei Tarkovsky on your film forum. A few
hours ago you downloaded *Solaris* off Pirate Bay and you are discussing it with the people on your film forum, the people you have been

discussing movies with online for almost two decades. Before you met Alice. Before things fell apart.

You notice you have a DM, the little notification bar at the top right-hand of the screen turning green to alert you that you have a new message. It's from someone named Shepitkogirl who has sent you a long list of Russian movies to watch. You shoot her back a DM thanking her for the list and to your surprise she answers back right away. The board is usually dead at this time of night. The board is dominated by overly opinionated Americans who worship Tarantino and at this time of night they should be sleeping. You ask Shepitkogirl if she has insomnia or if she's just European and she sends back a quick message.

LOL neither. russian, actually (Siberia!!1 brr). cool that ur into russian films. Not to many of us around here.

You don't know what to say to a Russian girl so you ask Shepitkogirl if she's in school for film and she answers that she's not in university yet, she's only 16. You wonder if Shepitkogirl should be telling you that she is 16 and that she lives in Siberia. You remember all that stuff on internet safety they tried to teach you when you were a kid. Don't tell strangers where you live seems like a pretty basic principle. You wonder if you should warn Shepitkogirl that you could be anyone, you could be a stalker, a pervert, a rapist, a predator. Instead you decide to look up Siberia on Wikipedia where you learn that Siberia isn't a city or even a province, but a huge district that encompasses most of Russia. To your great relief Shepitkogirl is safe in the anonymity of vast Siberian territory. The green indicator beside Shepitkogirl's name flicks off indicating that somewhere on the other side of the planet Shepitkogirl has closed a box or walked away from the computer to go do whatever Russian girls do. You're not sure exactly what that could be since everything you know about Russia is limited to Dostoyevsky and Tarkovsky. You spend the next two hours reading up on Siberia.

Guess where the coldest place on Earth is? you ask Alice when you finally log off and climb into bed. Her body is comfortably warm underneath the covers, but you keep your distance, positioning yourself as far away as you can on your side of the bed. You try and bask in the residual glow of Alice's warmth which has bled from her side of the bed over to yours.

I don't know, Alice says. In her half sleep she sounds friendly.

Come on, you say. Just guess.

Antarctica, she offers. This immediately puts you in a bad mood. You know instinctively that this is the right answer, but it wasn't the answer you were looking for. You hesitate for a moment, trying to figure out how to go back, how to rephrase the question, but it is too late, Alice has already rolled over on her side and is looking at you. She is more awake than her voice had indicated. Her eye has caught a source of light drifting through the window and sends a small twinkle out to you.

So? she asks. Am I right?

Let me start over, you say. What's the coldest city on Earth?

You have lost her. Alice rolls back over, her back to you again.

That's not what you asked.

I'm asking it now.

I'm tired. I don't know, okay? Just tell me.

Yakutsk, you say.

Yakutsk? Alice says. Is that in Russia? She sighs. I should have guessed Siberia.

You smile at the ceiling, privately gloating.

When you come down for breakfast Alice is sitting cross-legged on the kitchen island eating a bowl of cereal while reading the *Globe and Mail* on her laptop. Alice has a child's approach to furniture that you find disconcerting; she liked to nap on the big wide shelves of the library before you filled it with books, and sometimes you will find her tucked into a closet with her laptop or a book. Although Alice is two years older than you, her face is still as smooth and unlined as it was when you met her. The lines that trace across your forehead have been steadily growing since you were 13, and here is Alice, a grown woman with no lines. You have never seen Alice frown, but then you have never seen her smile in joy either. When she told you that you were going to be a father her face was as smooth as it always is, the only deviation from her normal expression a little more light in her eyes, the upturn of one corner of her mouth. You wonder why she is saving all her expressions. You wonder for who.

You watch her for a moment and then go upstairs hoping she never heard you. You get back under the warm covers and pretend to be asleep, opening your eyes every few minutes to check the alarm clock. In 10 minutes she will be out the door and on her way to work. You will be a few minutes late, but it will be worth it if you get to enjoy your breakfast alone.

You start reading everything you can on Yakutsk. You learn that it is only the coldest city on Earth for part of the year; in the summer the heat can climb all the way up to 38°C. You don't share this bit of information with Alice, you want to shield her from the disappointment, you want her to keep believing in Yakutsk as an ice city, frozen all year round.

In Yakutsk, you tell her later in bed, people leave their cars running for hours at a time so they don't freeze up.

When I was a little girl, Alice counters, my mom used to tell me she would send me to Siberia when I was being bad. I think she read *Crime and Punishment* too many times.

Have you noticed, she continues, her body slowly snaking over to your side of the bed. All Russian movies end with people being sent to Siberia to work in a gulag?

She reaches her hand out to touch your stomach and for a second you stop breathing and just let it rest there. Then, before you even quite know what you are doing, you have pulled away and are standing on the cold rug staring down at Alice who is looking up at you in confusion.

I'm going to go check on something, you say.

Sure, Alice says.

Alice doesn't ask what.

To make it seem like you are actually doing something, you go to your office where you turn on your computer and go to your film forum. You look for Shepitkogirl, but her online profile says she hasn't logged on in a week, the day you talked about *Solaris* and Russian movies and Siberia. Instead of going back to bed you download *The Ascent*, one of the movies Shepitkogirl recommended. You wonder if Alice is right and it will end with someone being shipped off to Siberia.

Helena thinks Yakutsk is a bad idea. Helena thinks that you should take Alice somewhere romantic like Paris or Venice, or at least somewhere people have heard of, like Amsterdam. Helena, like a xenophobe, seems to think that romance can only flourish in European locales. You tell Helena that Alice wants to go to Yakutsk with you, but Helena rolls her eyes, disbelieving. You tell Helena that your alternatives to Yakutsk are Tierra del Fuego, which Helena likes the sound of, until you tell her it is a remote archipelago, the southernmost in South America, or the Pitcairn Islands, which are only accessible by boat once every six months and boast a population of 50 souls. It's also known for a sexual abuse scandal which in the end implicated all the adults on the islands.

Considering your alternatives, Helena begins to warm to Yakutsk. To try to win her approval you tell Helena that Yakutsk museums have woolly mammoths that were perfectly preserved in the permafrost for millennia that have been dug out of the snow and mounted for display. When you were little and Helena was not, your mother used to bully her into taking you to the Museum of Nature where a trio of woolly mammoths (mother, father, and child you always thought) proudly guarded the parking lot. Somewhere there is a picture of Helena as a child, fiercely straddling the baby mammoth, hands on hips like an ice-age child warrior. There is a similar picture of you at the same age atop the baby mammoth, but in yours you are crying.

Before Helena hangs up she suggests therapy, which you try to laugh off. This is difficult because Helena is not joking. You feel bad, the way you always do when you are going to do something that disappoints Helena. You try to tell her that everything is okay and that everything is going to continue to be okay.

Helena asks if Alice is going to be okay, and when you don't answer right away her mind goes to the worst place. She mistakes your silence on the subject as a sign that Alice is an emotional train wreck when really all it means is that you don't know how to tell her that Alice is fine. That she never stopped being okay.

Shepitkogirl is thrilled that you loved *The Ascent*. She's also pleased that you have vowed to make your way through the rest of her list. In a misguided gesture of friendship she asks you to recommend a list of Canadian movies for her to watch. Not knowing what to say you suggest she start with Cronenberg, hoping that his filmography will keep her busy for a couple of weeks until you have time to actually watch enough Canadiana to form opinions. Shepitkogirl informs you that she already has a copy of *The Brood* and promises that she will have watched it by the next time you log on. You make a mental note to find and watch *The Brood* just as Alice walks through the door.

Whatcha doing? she asks as she comes towards you with her arms open. Halfway to you she changes her mind and leans over you, resting her chin on your head and peering at the screen.

Talking to a 16-year-old from Siberia, you say.

Travel advice? she asks.

You shake your head, which has the added effect of dislodging her chin from the top of your head.

Movies, you say.

Alice grew up watching TV and playing sports. She likes movies she can watch and then immediately forget about. Action, explosions, minimal dialogue. She considers any movie made five years ago ancient. She finds the idea of having opinions on European cinema bizarre, which you used to find charming.

Alice loses interest and walks upstairs to take a shower.

It is apparently easier to find David Cronenberg movies in Siberia than it is to find them in Canada. It is impossible to stream *The Brood*, and when, in desperation, you try to find a physical copy you balk at the price for a Criterion. You settle for pirating the film, downloading a version with Swedish subs hardcoded onto the screen. You ask Alice if she wants to watch it with you and she politely declines.

Horror films aren't really your thing, and neither is *The Brood*. After a few minutes you're tempted to turn it off, but Shepitkogirl is in the back of your head and so you keep watching. You are right in the middle of a yawn, counting down the minutes until the film ends, when Samantha Eggar parts her robe to reveal the strange tumoured fetus that she has been secreting there. You struggle for the mouse, meaning to hit the fast-forward button, but instead your cursor clicks on pause. For what feels like forever you are staring at the screen. Then you hear some music turn on downstairs and you fumble for the X button hurrying to dispel the image before Alice can see it. You feel very lucky that your wife didn't want to watch the movie with you.

When Shepitkogirl sends you a DM saying she didn't really like *The Brood*, you feel grateful that her one line doesn't beg for further conversation on the subject. You suggest she move on to '80s Cronenberg parroting a popular opinion on the film forum that this was when he hit his stride.

Alice wants to know how people survived in Yakutsk before the invention of electricity. You have been discussing how best to prepare for the freakish cold. Alice has brought forth the idea that if you both are too wimpish to brave the outside you become mole people and simply stay inside your hotel for the entire trip. Your throat closes up when she suggests this. You tell her that you are sure that there are tours for you to take.

Alice wonders how fast things freeze in Yakutsk in January.

What I really want to know, she confesses, laughing, is if I sneeze outside will my sneeze freeze?

You try to Google the question but come up with nothing.

Ask your 16-year-old Siberian, Alice suggests, and you promise that you will. Over and over again you type the question into the little DM window that holds the conversation between you and Shepitkogirl before erasing it. You don't know how to ask a question about sneezes in between suggesting depressing films. You don't know how to ask a question about sneezes without mentioning your wife, realizing that by introducing Alice you will be introducing the question of why you hadn't mentioned her earlier (which makes you look like a pervert even as you try to keep your conversations with Shepitkogirl as neutral and film focused as you can, even as you ignore that she has begun to sign her messages with a name, presumably her first one, that instantly renders her more human). You never ask Shepitkogirl if her sneezes freeze and Alice forgets all about it, just as you hoped she would.

The more you avoid talking to Alice about arctic sneeze freezes, the more the question resonates in your head. You learn that at −40°C a poured cup of water will freeze on its way to the ground. You can't wait to try this out in Yakutsk. You wonder if your tears would freeze instantaneously. You wonder if you were stabbed outside in Yakutsk if the stab wound or the cold would kill you first. You wonder if the blood would freeze inside you if you stayed outside long enough.

When you get home from work, Alice's coat is already on the coat rack, silently signifying that for once she has arrived home before you.

You call out for her and she shouts hello back from the master bath.

As you climb up the stairs you tell her that you went to see the travel agent who works in the same building as you. You are smug that she didn't even know where Yakutsk was.

Well, it's not exactly Rome, is it? Alice says.

The door is slightly ajar and you can see that she is dressed only in her underwear and bra.

You ask her why she is home so early.

I felt a little sick, she says with a shrug.

You push open the door to go inside and feel her forehead for any sign of fever. You see that she has been washing a pair of panties in the tub, using dish soap to scrub out the bloodstain. You remember that once, when you were trying to shut the window in her rickety old apartment, you cut your finger on the frame and tracked blood everywhere, on the floor, on her jeans, on your favourite blue shirt.

Don't worry, she had said, taking a bottle of dish soap and upending a generous amount on your shirt. Just watch. She rubbed the fabric together until the soap had worked itself up into a pure white lather and when she pulled her hands apart the stain had vanished.

How did you know that? you had asked her in wonder.

I'm a woman, she had laughed. I know how to deal with blood.

And here she is, dealing with blood again, her shoulders up, her arms crossed.

You see, or think you see, blood circling the drain.

It's normal, she says before you can say anything. This happens to me once a month for six days.

You shut your eyes against the residual blood in the tub, but this only brings back old images of Alice and blood.

It happened to me, to my body, she says walking towards you, trying to get you to look her in the eyes.

It happened to her. But it didn't.

You woke up and the sheets were wet. You reached out your arm to turn on the light and when you did you saw your fingertips were red with blood.

Alice, you said, you started your period, sweetie.

And then you both remembered, out of the fog of sleeplessness, that she wasn't supposed to be having periods anymore.

When you looked back at her the sheets were stained and heavy-wet with blood.

Alice had brought her hands up to her face and was examining the red which was sliding with sickening luxury down her fingertips towards her elbow.

Call 911, she said calmly.

And you did.

You thought that Shepitkogirl would be on your side when it came to Yakutsk, but you were wrong.

Ru crayʒ? Only true idiot would go there in winter. It's freʒing cold!

You send her a message back.

Too bad. Was hoping we could meet up, seeing as how we'll be in the same country and all.

Who are you talking to? Alice asks from her corner of the room. She has twisted herself up near the fire with a book.

The Siberian, you say in answer to her question.

I better be careful, she says, not looking up from her book. Next thing I know you'll have run off with the Siberian. Guess I'll have to find some balding 50-year-old on *World of Warcraft* to compete.

You smile at the joke, but you understand the message. You decide to stop talking to Shepitkogirl, at least for now.

Helena said that the best thing was to have another baby as quickly as possible. You told her that Alice wasn't ready and Helena put her hand on your arm and told you that she understood and that you had to be fair to Alice. You don't know how to tell her that Alice said the same thing verbatim to you before she had even stopped bleeding.

You were in the hospital with her, holding her hand in yours, wondering how someone could bleed that much and still live, trying to tell her it wasn't her fault and you didn't blame her. What you realized later, what you could never quite understand, was that she had never blamed herself at all. The doctors had told her that it was a much more common occurrence than most people liked to talk about and that it happened to women all the time. And she believed them.

It's a good thing we're Canadian, Alice says right before your winter mitts tumble off the top closet shelf and onto her head. We already own more than half the stuff we need for Yakutsk.

You put on a bright orange puffy coat that Alice's father gave you the one time you went hunting with him.

Alice is wriggling into the blue nylon snow pants you wore when you were 11. They fit her. She sees you in the puffy coat and starts to laugh. Kicking the mitts and scarves out of her way, she shuffles towards you, the nylon pants making a horrific zip-zip noise as her thighs rub together.

You try to ward her off, but before you know it, she has tackled you in a bear hug that you can barely feel because of the warm down and nylon between you.

Hesitantly, you try to wrap your arms around her.

Okay, stop, you say after a moment. I can't breathe like this.

You disentangle yourselves and continue to wade through all the ridiculous winter stuff, choosing with care the things you will take with you to Yakutsk.

The day after you came back from the hospital together you tried to do everything for Alice.

I'm fine, she kept insisting, but you were afraid of the icy pallor that had infected her skin, afraid that if you stopped doing things for her she would shrivel away and disappear along with the baby.

It wasn't a baby, Alice reminds you later on when you try to talk about it with her at night, in the same bed where it happened. It was a fetus. This happens all the time.

You started having nightmares about the blood shortly after. Alice held you in her arms after each one, stroking your sweaty hair, and whispering shh, shh, the echoes of a heartbeat. You asked her once if she dreamed about it too, but she said she didn't even remember any of it.

I can remember looking at my hands, she says, and I remember telling you to call 911, but I remember white, the white of the walls around my hands, and the white of the sheets. I don't remember any of the blood.

When you left the hospital you had to wheel Alice out in a wheelchair. They said it was standard procedure, but you didn't believe them, you were sure that it meant that Alice was still weak and fragile, still in danger. When you got to the car you insisted on lifting Alice out of the wheelchair and into the passenger seat, buckling her in like the child she had felt like in your arms. She kept telling you she was fine.

Every waking moment felt like hell, the briefest mentions of playgrounds, children, new furniture like barbed eruptions. If you felt like this, surely it must be worse for Alice who had had it happen inside her, inside her body.

When you got home you carried her across the threshold like a bride.

Don't move, you said as you deposited her (gently, gently) onto the couch.

I'll get you some water to go with your iron pill.

By the time you came back Alice had slouched over in a corner of the couch, her foot jiggling in time to the theme song from *The Simpsons*.

Thanks, sweetheart, she said as you handed her the glass, and then tilted her head back for a kiss.

You leaned down to kiss her back and then jerked your head away, the metallic smell of blood overwhelming your senses.

You okay? she asked, surprised.

You nodded, overwhelmed, and then sat down in a chair closer to the TV. The smell was gone, just as suddenly as it appeared.

You narrowed your eyes and tried to focus on the cartoon family in front of you.

Lately, when you grocery shop, or go to the bank, or go for a walk by the canal, crossing the street to avoid nosy neighbours who know what happened and want to interrogate you under the pretence of showing concern, when you sit on your corner of the couch trying not to breathe in, all the while aware of Alice, sitting on the farthest opposite end, all this time you are composing DMs to Shepitkogirl. You want to impress her with your knowledge of the golden '50s of Japanese cinema, your love of Lars von Trier, your prowess in having hunted down the entire oeuvre of Ousmane Sembène, your respect for French cinema's grand-mère, Agnès Varda. You think of all the Russian last names you know and you wonder which one of these might be hers. You think of signing your latest message to her with your real name in full, just casually dropping it where you normally write your username in the hopes that she will mimic your action the next time she writes to you. Each time you write to Shepitkogirl you begin with your real name, which you carefully delete, letter by letter, right before sending. You are aware of the possibility that something very bad might happen, and you don't know what to do about it.

I love you, you say as you are washing the dishes, an involuntary reflex from a different time.

Alice does not cover her surprise well.

I love you too, she says shyly and then tiptoes towards you and kisses you hesitantly on your shoulder. You submit to this because you know that it is your fault, that your thoughtlessness made her believe, at least for a moment, that things were better.

Her lips hesitate on your shoulder and you will yourself to stone, praying that she will feel the coldness of your muscles and walk away.

She does. When you are sure that she is gone, when you have heard the rustle of Alice in the living room, sorting through the old papers she is trying to get rid of, you resume washing the dishes as quietly as possible, hoping that Alice will forget that you are there at all.

When you are halfway through drying the dishes Alice begins to hum.

Everyone grieves in a different way, Helena told you, but this doesn't look like grieving to you.

Later that night, when Alice is in bed, you log onto your film forum looking for a message from Shepitkogirl.

GOODBYE, MELODY

LAST NIGHT I SAW MELODY.

You remember Melody, don't you? Or maybe not. She belongs to a time that was years and years ago, when we were the sort of little children who pretended we didn't still play with dolls.

After seeing her I went home and looked for the only picture I have with her in it, one of those class photos they take every year during grade school. My mother has dutifully preserved all of mine in an album so that by quickly flipping a few pages you can watch sweet children of four age crookedly into adolescence.

We were so pretty you and I. Perhaps it was only nostalgia, but in the picture everyone seemed pretty, even the ugly ones, even Melody. There was I (white cotton dress shrunk hopelessly in the wash) and there were you (with the shiny red shoes I silently coveted that whole entire year). And, separated from us by two rows of feral cherubs who seemed to think that smiling was simply an aggressive exposure of the teeth, there was Melody.

Poor sad sack Melody.

You know, I miss you now that you are not here, for we used to have our own coded language, a language built up from a childhood of whispers and imagined persecution and not-so-secret secrets. I miss you especially every time I look a person up and down and declare them to be a Melody. No one ever knows what I'm talking about, and I am always forced to explain that Melody was the girl who cried during dodgeball if the ball so much as rolled in her direction. And though they understand the reference (who had a childhood without a Melody?) it is never quite the same as if you'd been there to sneer with me.

Now that I think about it, what I really remember is how she used to cry and cry and cry. Of course, once she made the mistake of exposing this curious tick we never casually passed the ball to her again. No, we whipped it at her face, arms, shoulders, thorax, tibia, places I couldn't yet name but could certainly target. The nape of her neck, I seem to remember, was of particular concern to her. She would keep her hands protectively crossed over it, her elbows raised so that she looked like a flightless bird, as the ball arched towards her in an easy slope. Do you know I had forgotten until just now that we used to make a game of it, 10 points for the face, 100 for the neck? I do not remember who the all-time champion was, except that it was neither you nor me. I think it was that tall boy with the glasses who later moved to Australia (you must not forget to tell me his name if you can recall it).

But heartless as we were, I think we might have forgiven her pigeonish stupidity during gym if it had not been for my pen. Even if you have forgotten Melody, I am sure you still remember the pen. That gleaming source of so much trouble which belonged to my father and carried a special weight because it was made of real gold. I used to watch with envy as he signed his name to cheques, its glimmer and lustre inspiring my lust much in the way that crows covet tinfoil. It was always a special occasion when he let me hold it in my little hands, letting me feel its solid mass on my palms before he took it away, tucking it safely back into its case. I knew, even back then, that I was too young, too stupid, too careless to own such a beautiful thing. But I wanted it and I took it and, as you no doubt remember, I inevitably lost sight of the thing the way careless children inevitably do.

One of my clearest memories from childhood is from that time. You comforting me outside the gates of the school because the pen had been stolen is one of my dearest memories of us together.

I will always be grateful for the fact that you never questioned whether or not Melody really took it. My word was enough for you, and my word was certainly enough for me, for I felt, with something less like intuition and more like rabid faith, that Melody had taken it.

I think the searches began sometime after that. It seems to stretch out forever in my mind, a time unceasing where we (not just you and me, but a crowd of now-faceless others) pinned Melody to the wall before class and rifled through her things.

As children we already had the strangest ideas of justice. I distinctly remember you encouraging me to take things as compensation for the gold pen: tin pencil coffers, candy, and a beautiful 50-plus pack of Crayola crayons. And because I was generous I used to take things for you and the others too. I have a funny memory of you choosing a dandelion-coloured crayon out of my (Melody's?) crayon box which you kept in your pocket and used to absentmindedly lick from time to time, forgetting that the sunny lemon shade did not correspond to the sweetness of rock candy but to the bitter taste of wax.

It was possibly around the time that I confiscated the crayons that we discovered the pen. It had, ridiculously enough, fallen into a hole in the lining of my book bag. Being judicious I called a secret council (do you remember?) which we held over a feast of juice and crackers, scribbling in our illiterate children's scrawl the different points for and against continuing the searches. I do not remember all the things we wrote at that silly summit, but I do remember that we decided that the searches should not stop. After all, it was only dumb luck that I had discovered the pen midsemester and not during summer, or some later far-off time when Melody was not right there in front of us. Melody, taunting us with her blank face and her endless store of crayons and markers which seemed to hold hostage within their plastic confines all the colours of the world.

That awful face. If I think about it, it is really a wonder that I managed to remember her last night after so much time had passed. Most of the time we spent with her as children we were rifling through her things and I never troubled myself to look up at her face. I can remember the way she used to suck on her hair, or the awkward elbow wings she made, but her face . . .

The only time I ever remember really looking at her face was the time we pushed her down the stairs. Tumbling backwards, utterly graceless, the arc of her back as she went curving over each step; yes, that was the only time her mushroom face ever took on any expression. We all saw, we all knew, that though it seemed impossible the moment would end, it was only a matter of time before she shattered to the floor. I believe I laughed before she landed because of the way her arms flailed about for the hand rail or a helping hand. What a heartless young girl I was to find the humour as her legs flew up into the air, her eyes and mouth rounded in surprise as gravity pulled her mercilessly down.

You know, I do not understand why we were never punished, for we were such bad little girls. I understand why no one ever told; they hated her. And I never told because I would have done anything for you, as you would have for me. What I will never understand is why *she* never told. I suppose it would have made little difference anyway since by then her parents had decided to pull her out of our school. Secretly though, I always felt if such a thing had been done to me (though who would have dared!) I would have screamed the guilty party's name over and over and not rested till their breast had been emblazoned with a blood-red P for pusher.

I do confess I felt a tiny twinge of something when I heard that she was leaving school. I had become so fond of those crayons, and not knowing when or where I would get a fresh supply, I regretted giving so many away (though not to you, never to you).

Do you know, out of all the silly things we did together, I can never remember why we did that? We must have been very angry I think, but I can't remember why.

I could not stop staring at her as she was walking down the street last night and at first I did not understand. Then her ankle twisted and her arms spread wide as she fought for balance. Her mouth made a tiny pink *o* of surprise and I knew who she was. She did not go down this time.

I raised my hand to wave at her and then thought better of it. You will be interested to know that she is very tall now, and even somewhat pretty-looking, though of course she still walks with a limp.

THE SINGING KEYS

FOR THREE MONTHS, when Margarita was 16, the world shifted and everything made sense.

If she had known that it was only going to last a season she would have done things differently. She would have learned languages. Russian, maybe, the language of Gogol and Chekhov and Tolstoy and Pushkin. Or French, the language of Proust and Dumas and Duras and Zola, or Spanish, the language of Paz and Rulfo and Neruda and perhaps, more importantly, her father's mother tongue.

She could have become a woman of science or a woman of war. She could have rearranged the universe to better suit her liking, but she didn't. The world was unfolding before her in a way that seemed as simple and logical as the addition of one plus one and she thought she had all the time in the world to watch things play out to their inevitable conclusions.

It wasn't all regret and waste. In those three months Margarita fell in love, for the first time, with Alastair McDean, the school star.

Alastair was a drama student whom everyone in school had collectively fallen in love with two years earlier after seeing him perform a selection of *Hamlet* monologues during his grade 10 student showcase.

Margarita was not a drama student, she was a vocal student, an indifferent one, and in the early years of high school she had been berated so thoroughly for the mediocrity of her voice that sometimes the sound of it, the thinness of it, the lack of quality, was enough to reduce her to tears. Yet something strange happened in those three months. Sitting in the padded vocal room, running her scales, she understood of the workings of her own vocal cords. She could hold notes with a power and a purity which she had never had before. A month after the sense-making began, a few days after she and Alastair kissed for the first time in the auditorium control room, Margarita's music teacher, Mrs. Leith, latched on to the fact that something magical was happening. Mrs. Leith was a failed singer of undetermined age, with dark hair streaked through with white and perfect pitch. The students called her the King Maker after her success in sending her favourite students to the conservatories of her choice. Margarita had never been worthy of her notice before, but after she heard Margarita singing alone in the vocal practice room she rapped on the window with her ring finger and asked Margarita to stay after school. Thus began the extra lessons, first once, then twice a week.

It was quite something to hear Margarita's new voice. She was a small girl with a plain round face and a flat wide nose, who before had had a voice clear as crystal and just as liable to break. Before Mrs. Leith she now stood with her hands clasped in front of her and sang with depth. Sometimes the sounds she produced were so fantastic that Mrs. Leith would end the sessions early so as not to frighten Margarita with the tears of wonder that clouded her eyes.

At the end of three months Mrs. Leith began to ask Margarita what her plans for the future were. Margarita had planned to follow

Alastair to McGill, where he would be going in the fall and where she would join him a year later, but Mrs. Leith told her these plans were all wrong and as Mrs. Leith talked, Margarita listened. Mrs. Leith wanted Margarita to apply to Juilliard, something she had recommended to only two of her students during her 30-year teaching career. One of the singing coaches was coming to teach a masterclass in the spring. He was a friend of Mrs. Leith and she had provided him with a recording, secretly made, of one of Mrs. Leith and Margarita's private sessions. Margarita had been invited to the masterclass to sing. She would be the youngest student there by far.

To Margarita, who only a few months earlier had been unloved and unnoticed, this did not seem so much an honour but what she was rightfully due.

As Margarita prepared for her masterclass the world continued to fall into place. Everything seemed so easy, every thing seemed to speak its purpose and its secrets to her. Then she began to hear things.

A certain low-grade tintinnabulation began to haunt her. At night she would wake from her room and prowl the house, searching for the source of the gentle ringing. When she was at school or alone with Alastair in his home she never heard it. Yet every time she returned home the ringing would begin, sometimes loudly, sometimes more a suggestion than a noise. Her mother and father couldn't hear a thing, which didn't worry Margarita because she thought of them as old and practically dead. But when her younger sister, Vera, couldn't hear it either, Margarita began to worry.

Her father took her to the doctor's office at a time when he should have been at work and she should have been having a singing lesson with Mrs. Leith. In his car the noise was especially loud, and when her father got out of the car to pump gas, Margarita had to place her hands over her ears to try to dim the piercing whistle. When she leaned forward, in agony, the noise only seemed to get louder. It was coming from the engine, no, it was coming from the glove compartment box. When Margarita opened up the glove compartment there, mixed in with her father's insurance papers, were a pair of keys she had never seen before. And the keys were singing.

Poor thing, her father said, cradling her in his arms as they waited to be seen by the doctor. My poor little girl.

The doctor looked first in Margarita's left ear and then in her right. The doctor asked Margarita a lot of questions about when the ringing had begun, what it sounded like, and how often she heard it. Though the doctor never asked, Margarita explained how important it was that she be able to hear as she was a singer. The doctor nodded and then typed a note in Margarita's chart.

But then just in the car now, on our way over, it just—

Margarita brought her hands together and then pushed her fingers apart. A vanishing act. No more ringing.

It happens sometimes, the doctor told Margarita's father. Come back if it starts up again and I'll recommend an otologist.

As her father and the doctor talked to each other Margarita slipped one of her hands into her pocket and ran her fingers over the teeth of first one and then the other key. They were still singing to her.

That evening she slipped out of her home and rather than meet Alistair she walked to the hardware store and had them make a copy of the singing keys. As they were being copied they started to sing a new song, a song of directions to the locks they fit in. They sang this new song to Margarita as she came back home and stole her father's car key to slip the keys back into his car. The key copies didn't sing at all, didn't even speak, and though she knew it was dangerous, these new treacherously mute keys were the ones Margarita put back in her father's glove compartment.

Every day since she had turned 13 and gotten into the special high school that offered things like drama and vocal, Margarita had woken up early and taken two buses to get from her home, in the heart of the city, to the high school, in the suburbs. But that day, instead of heading south to her school, she took a bus to the east, to see the locks where the keys belonged. She had to get off the bus in an unfamiliar place, where all the houses looked the same and the streets twisted into each other in a strange labyrinth, but the singing keys told her which way to go and where to turn.

At last she arrived at an ugly hulking tenement building made of dirtying grey concrete. There were balconies running up and down the building and each one was crowded with its own unique blend of items, laundry, and discarded furniture that had been deemed unfit to fill the apartments proper. The pavement outside the building was strewn with cigarette butts and gum. From somewhere up high, the angry voice of a man belted through the air shouting, You bitch! You fucking bitch—

A woman with some grocery bags wheezed past Margarita, and Margarita, seeing that she was headed inside, darted forward to the entrance of the building and held the first door open. The woman looked at her suspiciously and then passed through, put down her bags, and punched in the door code. When the buzzer went off, Margarita rushed to hold that door open too and this time the woman smiled at her, a hesitant, broken little thing that looked as if it cost the woman too much to give. In the elevator, the woman pushed the nine button, its numbered face half-burnt away, and Margarita tapped the five, the way the keys told her to.

On the fifth floor the keys began to sing louder than ever and the closer she got to the locks, the louder they sang. When she at last reached the correct door she put a key in the handle, unlocked it, and then put the other in the top lock and unlocked that. As she placed each key in its allotted slot, it stopped singing and issued a deep sigh of contentment. For a minute Margarita didn't know what to do, the silence overwhelming her. Then she pulled them out and the singing started again.

There was nowhere to go but forward and so Margarita walked into the apartment. It was not a nice place. It smelled synthetically floral and underneath that was the distinct odour of food left to rot. The bare white walls had streaks of dirt here and there. With each step Margarita took there was an unpleasant and sandy-sounding little crunch from her shoe against the grit on the floor. There were heaps of laundry on the couch, and Margarita went to it and touched the cheap clothes of the woman who lived there. Her threadbare jeans, her nylon blouses.

So the woman was poor. Margarita walked through the living room looking carefully at her tacky things. She did not even know that she was looking for anything in particular until she found it, a picture of her father with the woman who presumably lived in the apartment, a picture of them laughing into the camera. Her father's arms were wrapped around the woman in a way that was intimate and unmistakable, his cheek pressed up close to hers. She picked up the picture to examine it more closely but when she put it back she misjudged her aim and it clattered to the floor so loudly Margarita was sure it was broken. For a moment she stood still waiting to feel the pain from the shards of glass embedded in her flesh. When she finally gathered up the courage to look she realized there were no shards, no broken glass at all. The cheap frame had survived and what she had thought was glass was just plastic. She picked it up and put it back where she thought she had found it.

Hello?

In real life the woman from the picture looked older and more tired than her photographic self. She, or someone she had not paid very much, had attempted to dye her hair blond but had only succeeded in turning it a burnt orange. She had a baby on her hip and the baby looked at Margarita and smiled. In that smile were echoes of Vera when she had been a newborn.

Do I know you?

There was a phone in the woman's other hand and her thumb was poised over the keypad. Margarita no longer felt certain of anything but she would have bet that the woman had already dialled at least the 9 of 911.

I'm Jorge and Elena's daughter.

Oh.

All the fight rushed out of the woman all at once. She moved her thumb quickly to end the call and then threw the phone on the couch, where it landed softly amongst the clothes, and then stood there, not quite able to meet Margarita's eyes.

Margarita kept looking at her and then looking at the baby who looked like Vera and couldn't think of a thing to say.

Shouldn't you be in school, honey? the woman finally asked.

Yeah.

Do you want a ride?

Even though Margarita would not have known the way to the woman's house without the singing keys, the woman knew the way to Margarita's school without being told.

Like her home, the woman's car was cheap and ugly, the sides rusting out and the seat patched in places with duct tape, but the car seat in which she placed Margarita's brother was new and expensive.

Are you Vera? the woman asked as they stopped at a red light.

No, Margarita said. She felt offended that this woman knew Vera's name and, knowing it, did not know enough to know that Vera was only 12 years old.

Margarita then, the woman said. Margarita who sings.

But she must have sensed something of Margarita's anger for she didn't say anything more. The light turned green and that was that.

By the time they reached the school it wasn't even midday. As she opened the car door, Margarita turned to the woman and said, I would prefer if we pretended this day never happened. The woman opened her mouth to say something and then shut it again and simply nodded and Margarita felt a wave of relief wash over her that she could be done with the whole wretched day.

Thank you, Margarita said and then felt ashamed. She should have spit on the woman. She felt her lack of loyalty to her mother like a poison deep in her bones.

Instead she turned to say goodbye to the baby who was gurgling prettily in the back seat and then just as abruptly lurched towards the passenger side door and, still half in the car, threw up on the sidewalk. The bile that spewed from her was textured like the oatmeal she had eaten that morning and was flavoured with an acid that burned her mouth and made her eyes water. She could feel the woman behind her, rubbing her back, murmuring words of comfort. A comfort that unsettled. Margarita closed her eyes accepting the woman's hands on her back because she couldn't do anything else, couldn't even push her away and scream like she wanted to. When she felt steady enough she climbed out of the car, slamming the door behind her as she went. She never turned back.

At home Vera was the first one to greet her.

You're in big shit, Vera said, bouncing up and down looking malicious and nothing like her bright, dumb, baby self.

The school called because you missed *half* a day.

What is wrong with you? Margarita's mother said as she came out of the kitchen.

Her anger dissipated as Margarita began to cry, as she walked into her mother's welcoming arms and clung to her.

It's all this singing nonsense, isn't it? her mother said as she cradled Margarita. You're just a kid, I don't know why that woman keeps putting all that pressure on you. I don't want you to go to Juilliard anyway. I'd miss you too much.

Her mother put her to bed early and Margarita lay there for a long time with tears sliding down her cheeks listening to the bed and the dresser and the walls and the ceiling all talking. Every book was vomiting its contents at her in hushed undertones and she wanted to listen to them all, but she could only hear a word or two before her attention was caught by something else. And over it all the keys were singing their beautiful directions to the blond woman's house, chanting them over and over in such a way that Margarita couldn't stop listening. She lay there listening to them all until very early in the morning when she had chewed her lip raw and the metallic taste of her own blood seeped into her mouth.

No more, Margarita begged. I don't want to know anything anymore.

The books were the first to hush, and then the house, and then the bed. Margarita fell asleep at last, just as the sun was beginning to rise, to the sound of the keys singing very, very softly for her alone.

When she finally woke there were two notes, both from her mother. The first told Margarita that in consideration of her hard work and the stress she was under she was being given the privilege of having a mental health day. The second was a note, signed and dated, excusing Margarita from her previous absence at school.

It was not as fun to stay at home as she would have imagined. She watched movies until her eyes ached and ate the cookies she knew Vera was saving for herself. But no matter where she wandered in the house she could hear the keys singing softly up in a drawer in her room.

It was always busy downtown, even midday when everyone was supposed to be at work. Margarita got off the bus at Parliament along with a crowd of tourists wearing bucket hats and backpacks, who ran straight through the gates towards the Eternal Flame. She broke away from the pack and turned left. She walked past Library and Archives and kept going until she was on the bridge to Hull.

The traffic across Portage Bridge was unrelenting, but aside from Margarita, the only pedestrian she saw was a lone jogger who quickly passed her. The river's current was strongest at the part where there was a little tourist sign and Margarita pretended to read the whole sign as the cars rushed past her, her hand in her pocket wrapped around the keys. It was hard to hear the keys over the sound of the cars and rushing water, but she could hear them anyway, hear them giving her directions in their beautiful voices.

When the keys were almost done their song she leaned over the railing pretending to admire the water. The current below was hypnotically violent, no wave or twist the same. She had almost let the keys slip out of her palm when she heard them change their tune. They began to sing another more frantic song, telling her that they still had so much to impart, promising her spitefully that she would never know any of it if she let them go.

She would be ordinary, they told her. She would be dull. Alastair would leave her. When she went to the masterclass her rich new voice would abandon her, falling away like smoke in the wind and with it would go Mrs. Leith and her patronage, her Juilliard connections.

It would be just like before—

And she tipped her hand and watched them fall prettily into the great white foamy waves which swallowed them whole.

AN OCCUPATION

PANIC. A DOOR. A door off its frame half an inch.

Keys in hand, Isa stared at the door that was supposed to separate the world from her possessions. She closed her eyes and counted to ten, gave up somewhere around seven. People all around the world were breathing in their first or last breaths. Somewhere someone was having the worst day of their entire life. And that someone was not her. Because she had left the door open herself. Because she was standing in front of the wrong door. Because it was only half an inch and what was a gap of half an inch in a world which itself was infinitesimal, smaller than the finest grain of dust in comparison with the universe which contained it.

She opened her eyes. The door, her door, was still open by half an inch. Panic.

She prodded the door open with a quick jab of her finger, unwilling to touch the thing for any longer than that. It swung open easily and immediately she saw the gold gleam of the deadbolt jutting out, vulgar and erect, the strike plate lying on the floor among bits of door frame.

It must have fallen there after it was ripped from the wall. Ripped by the force of someone pushing their way in.

Panic.

She called her mother.

Darling, her mother said in a voice too sensual to possibly be meant for her.

Mommy, Isa crashed in before the voice could betray itself any further. I've been robbed.

A silence grew up between them, pitch-black and pouring thick and toxic over everything.

Mommy? Isa said. Mommy?

Who is this? her mother said at last and hearing her speak was bittersweet.

It's Isa, Isa said. The lock is broken. I don't know—I don't know what's missing.

I can't hear—I can't— For God's sake, her mother stuttered and then there was a silence through which Isa strained to hear. She concentrated so fully, giving her entire body over to the listening, that when she finally heard the dial tone she dropped her phone, shocked by the abruptness of its inhuman sound.

Isa picked her phone off the floor, scrambled at buttons, and redialled.

The customer you have dialled is currently not available, a woman's automated voice told her, please try your call again later. L'abboné que vous tantez de joindre, a man's voice took over, est actuellement en l'impossibilité de répondre—

Isa, coming to her senses, hung up and dialled 911.

Take your time, the police officer said, one hand hovering near Isa's waist. When they had first entered the apartment, she had felt a wave of nausea and backed up in revulsion, colliding against his body with a violence that surprised them both.

She thought that she would have felt less disoriented if she'd come in and found the entire apartment filled with water, bloated books and water-logged debris floating strangely in rivulets that should not have been there. If she had walked through her apartment door and entered into a strange new life on Mars it would have made more sense, held more meaning, than whatever was occurring now.

Because when she had entered everything had looked so different from the way she had left it, disgusting and horrible and new, and yet, when they went back in, she could not point at any one thing, at any singular object, and say there, that thing right there is not how I left it.

And maybe everything looked to be in the same disordered order it had been when she had gone out, but there was a difference in the way the books were stacked and the way her clothes were tossed, even if they aped the way she had left them that morning, casting the same shadows as if they were not in some way fundamentally changed.

Isa shuddered. Everything looked touched, but when her eye settled on an object, she could not say with certainty that it was not exactly the way she had left it.

And this was somehow worse than entering a place in which her things had been tossed back and forth with little regard, like so much debris. Isa thought of strange hands carefully brushing the edge of her desk and roaming fingertips running lightly over the keys of her keyboard, keys which her own fingers touched with purpose and meaning every day. Strange bodies sitting gently in her chairs and lying softly in her bed, breathing in her air and seeing all that she saw now.

That's odd, the policeman said.

Isa looked at where he was pointing and when her eye settled she saw nothing that was odd and all that was ordinary.

What?

They just left your computer right there.

They looked at her computer and Isa felt something strange and hard flip inside her stomach.

The bedroom, she said, walking jerkily towards it. She stumbled over a bra she had discarded on the floor the night before, bent down and picked it up, and then dropped it down again, nervously thinking that surely she shouldn't touch things at the scene of the crime.

Something she knew from TV procedurals and now, she supposed, from life.

My jewellery.

The police officer hovered in the doorway as she rushed through her room. Here too everything had been curiously changed, and yet nothing had been disturbed. It was the air, Isa thought as her eyes scanned the room, refusing to settle on any one thing. Aliens had come and taken her away and brought her to this facsimile of her apartment in which they had carefully recreated every part of her life to the point that it was unsettlingly, erroneously correct.

Your bed, it was left like that? The police officer pointed at the duvet pouring off the edge of the bed onto the floor.

Yes, Isa said, a little embarrassed. That was me. I did that.

She went to the juvenile floral jewellery box she still used and yanked the drawers open, recklessly upturning them on the bed and pawing through the tangled chains, searching and searching for what was missing. As she moved her hands and separated the jewellery into piles, her actions took on a more and more frantic edge as rings, bracelets, charms, necklaces, all, all were accounted for. It was only on a second pass that she realized what was missing.

It's gone, she said at last when she was satisfied and sure.

Yeah? the police officer said, the relief in his voice almost as sharp as her own.

My bracelet, it was a present from my father, it had, had an engraving, a date, it was, let me, it was—

Let me get the form, he said and left her alone in the room full of things no longer her own.

She wrote the official report with an unsharpened pencil, the best she could find in the moment. As she wrote on and the nub grew flat and blunt, her words ran together in ill-formed half sentences, her handwriting regressing back to a childish, indecipherable scrawl.

The policemen left shortly after that. They did not promise that they would find her bracelet, but then again she never expected them to.

She kept trying to make things right again. Every stack of books or pile of pens, every arrangement of everything mocked her with its composition. She could not tell if things had always been that way or if someone else had made them so—she reshuffled everything in order to replace the doubt she felt with dead certainty.

Every day when she went looking for something and could not find it, she wondered if she had simply misplaced it or if it had been taken. She took to keeping a list of all those objects and then crossing them off when the item was found.

That first night, she had been filled with such exhaustion and dread that she had collapsed onto her bed and fallen into a deep dreamless sleep. In the morning she discovered what looked like the smudge of a shoeprint on the edge of her comforter and so she spent the next evening wearing latex gloves, shoving her clothes, her bedding, her intimate apparel into trash bags which she emptied into the basement laundry machines, careful not to let any of the cloth touch her skin.

An hour later when she came downstairs she found her things lying in a damp pile on top of the washing machine, her underwear gnarled and exposed at the very top. She felt like she was the victim of a great cosmic joke. She washed her things again.

A note on her door informed her that the super wanted to have a word with her. Sitting in the super's spacious apartment, a smoky atmosphere clouding around her, Isa felt a delightful light-headed high.

Twelve, the super said, pointing a finger at her.

Isa, Isa corrected.

Yes, exactly, the super said, waving her hand and unintentionally dispelling more smoke in Isa's direction. It burst over her like a foul cloud and Isa felt a trembling begin in her legs. If she stood up right at that moment she was sure she would fall down.

We all feel just terrible about what happened to you, the super began. She shoved a plate of digestive cookies into Isa's face and Isa waved a no with her hand, using the gesture to try to innocently dissipate some of the gathering smoke crowded around her.

You know this is a nice, quiet building, the super continued.

Yes.

And you yourself are a nice, quiet girl. Why, I remember the first time I ever saw you I said to myself, Now there's a girl who won't cause any trouble. A good, clean girl. I would rather rent to a girl a hundred times over than a man—

Yes, Isa said.

Focus on a fixed point, Isa told herself. Focus on the bookshelf, focus on the book behind her head.

And it's not that I blame you, the super continued. But I would prefer you keep from mentioning it to the other tenants. They might panic, you see. Panic over nothing. And then I would have to show the apartment, get new tenants. And it's not that I mind that, you see. That's my job and I'm proud of it. But it's impossible to find people who want to move in the winter. I defy you to find—

S-U-R, Isa began spelling out the title, desperate for the interview to end, unsure of how much more would be required of her. F-A-C-I-N-G and then it was like having a blindfold removed from her eyes because the whole title pressed itself into her mind at once and she realized that it was her book.

I'm fine, Isa said, before she really was. The super was leaning over her, breathing smoky breath directly up Isa's nostrils.

Your eyes just rolled up in your head, the super said, her voice full of wonder. Just slid out of the chair like it was nothing.

Could I please, Isa cleared her throat a little, stared straight ahead at the ceiling which was really all she could see from her angle on the floor. Could I please have a glass of water?

The super heaved herself up off her haunches with a soft grunt and retreated to the kitchen. Isa, half standing and half crawling, made her way to the bookshelf and sloppily plucked the book out, shuffling the other books around to cover the gap left behind.

She had just enough time to slip it into her handbag before the super was back, offering muggy tap water with a white cloud unfurling itself slowly within the liquid, its own separate atmosphere.

Actually, I'm fine, Isa said, stumbling backwards and refusing the water, wondering where she had put that policeman's card so she could tell him she knew who had taken her things, who had her bracelet. The whole time she was stumbling backwards, she wondered only if her face would betray her.

I won't mention a word to the other tenants. Just like you said. No need for panic.

Inside her apartment, Isa was filled with joyous abandon, rooting around until she found the card with the police officer's name and number printed on it. As she dialled, she wondered what would happen to the super and then decided she didn't care. She flipped through the book she had taken as the phone rang, fumbling till she found where the inscription would be. To Isa, it would say—only when she got the pages unstuck there was nothing on them. Smooth and undisturbed as if fresh from the printer.

An automated message told her to punch in the extension or hold please. Isa ended the call and let the phone slide out of her hands as she clutched at the book and examined its edges worn in places her own book was not. She went to her bookshelf and found her book, right where she had left it.

So. So no one had taken her book. So she had taken someone else's. Well, her bracelet was gone, there was still that at least, Isa thought looking around wildly at the things which were hers which no longer felt like things she had ever seen before, let alone things that she had any dominion over.

She slid the super's copy beside her own. She didn't quite know what else to do with it.

Isa found the bracelet the same day she found out that the man in the apartment beside her, Number Eleven, was telling people that he had heard the whole thing, had seen the whole thing unfold. *Unfold* was the word he was using, as if he were a spectator watching a flower blossom.

She heard it from the woman downstairs, Number Eight, who came over without warning and invited herself to stay for a cup of tea.

What happened was a tragedy, Eight said with a smile which would have meant more if she hadn't just barged into Isa's apartment and sat down among her things as if she owned them.

Did she own them? Isa wondered. Was this Eight's apartment? No, that was ridiculous. That was her clock right there, set an hour behind because Isa had never reset it for daylight saving.

Horrific, Eight continued, as her eyes ping-ponged around the apartment.

Thank you, Isa said, feeling the beginning of a headache sprouting somewhere deep within her. She raised a hand to her forehead in exaggeration, a woman imitating a woman having a headache even though her own was becoming realer by the second, hoping that Eight would get the hint. She didn't.

It could have happened to any of us, Eight said, eyeing the crumbs that speckled the kitchen table.

It would be alright, Isa thought, if she just quietly looked and judged, but no, Eight had to crane her neck, had to bug her eyes out, had to be, in general, as unsubtle as possible. She had actually started to sweep up the crumbs into a little pile at the edge of the table. It was almost, but not quite, unbearable.

What did he take, anyway? Eight wanted to know.

A bracelet, a silver bracelet, Isa said at the same time as she opened a drawer looking for tea and found her silver bracelet crowded beside some pencils.

Isa slammed the drawer shut on this perverse sense of kismet, forced herself to smile at Eight, and told her she had no tea bags left after all.

Don't worry about it, Eight said, even as Isa grabbed her by her watery bicep and led her briskly towards the door.

But wait a minute, Isa said, yanking her back across the threshold, the door gaping wide. Eight flinched and Isa wondered when she had turned into the sort of person who pushed around elderly women. Aliens, she decided. It was the only reasonable explanation.

Yes, dear? Eight said it like she was frightened of her, like maybe Isa was going to manhandle her back into the kitchen and chop her into little bits and bake her into a cake. Isa resented it.

How did you know—how did you even know about what happened? I didn't tell anyone. The super said—

Oh, but everyone knows, Eight said looking confused at Isa's confusion.

What are you talking about?

It's that man beside you, in number 11, you know? He's been telling everyone about how he saw the whole thing with his own two eyes. It's all he ever talks about, says he got a real good look, Eight was saying just as Isa loudly interrupted her with a goodbye and pushed her out of her apartment and shut the door in her face.

She could hear Eight shuffling around indignantly in the hallway for a while and then the scraping of slippers against floor whispering away, signifying retreat, defeat.

She went back to the kitchen drawer and withdrew the bracelet. She now remembered tossing it in there a long, long time ago when she had been cleaning up the counter, shoving everything haphazardly into the nearest drawer.

The inscription on the back read To my little Isabelle. Love, Daddy.

Isa told herself she was glad it had not been stolen.

Isa thought it might be nice to bring over some pastries or cookies or something so she went to the grocery store and bought some tarts with anemic crusts. She transferred them onto a plate before going over and knocking on Eleven's door.

Eleven had lived there for decades, certainly before Isa's time and maybe before everyone else's. He looked straight into her face as strange words came stuttering out of her mouth. A series of awkward introductions that went nowhere. In the end, all it took was her thrusting the tarts in his face and he ushered her into his apartment, opening the door wide and placing a hand on her forearm to guide her inside.

She found herself sitting shell-shocked in an armchair as he bit into the tart, crumbs flying everywhere. His apartment was an echo of her own, same closets and lighting fixtures, the radiators crowding into inconveniently placed outlets the same way hers did. Only the whole place was bare, the walls so white it ached to look at them.

There was nothing remotely personal in the room. Even the few pieces of furniture looked strangely new and untouched, not a scratch or mark on them. Like a laboratory. Like the set of a sci-fi film in which the heroes visit space. A moon colony. Isa was on the moon.

You want to know about the thief, Eleven said spraying crumbs everywhere before Isa had found the courage to speak up again. It wasn't a question.

Yes, I—

I saw everything, he interrupted.

Everything within his vicinity was now littered with debris and Isa thought how strange it was that this neat little man was such a disgusting eater.

Smashed in the door with a few quick throws of the shoulder. Didn't stay there too long.

And how long, Isa wondered, did he consider not too long? Had it been a polite break-in of only a few seconds, a few minutes, as if everything had been planned out in advance, what to touch, what to take, what to leave? Had it been a series of frantic minutes, adrenaline pumping as things were picked up and then put down again? Had it been difficult to decide what to take? Had they searched in places so private that Isa herself could no longer hope to remember what had been stored inside of them?

The only thing that Eleven had on his walls was a calendar with all the days so far lived faithfully crossed off. The picture for March was a naked woman straddling a motorcycle, her legs spread pornographically.

Isa crossed her own legs and leaned forward. Eleven leaned forward as well, like they were all friends here.

But did you tell the police—

He leaned back abruptly.

I don't get myself involved in that sort of thing.

But if you saw what was taken—

Might have been her boyfriend for all I know.

But I don't—and even if I did, all the more reason to—

That girl, he says leaning in again, flicking his tongue so that it smacked wetly against his bottom lip, has different men running in and out of there at all hours of the night.

But no, I don't, Isa found herself saying. I don't have a boyfriend at all.

Clinging to the inaccuracy as if by curing him of this falsity she could make him understand her.

For a minute Isa and Eleven looked into each other's eyes, humbled by their mutual ignorance, their complete inability to comprehend each other. It was a moment in which anything was possible, a moment in which they could have chosen to implode like supernovas or juggle. It could have been a fantastic anything and Isa was upset when she blinked and the moment was over. Eleven's face began to turn a strange purple as he realized who she was and in the end the only thing that did happen was that Eleven grabbed her by the forearm and led her out of his apartment calling her a crazy troublemaker, a bad girl, a liar.

But did you see what was taken? she asked as he closed the door in her face. Can't you just tell me what was taken?

She slapped her palm against the door again and again and was crushed that the weight of it, the force and the violence of everything she felt and said and wanted to say, translated into a muted slap and a stinging pain that hurt only her.

GIRL ON THE METRO

BY THE TIME NATASHA stepped onto the metro car, the girl had settled into a comfortable kneeling position her shins flush with the dirty floor. If it hadn't been for the loose roll of her head as it rocked from side to side, swayed along by the motion of the tracks, Natasha would have guessed she was praying.

She sat down in an empty seat near the doors, from where she could easily slide her eyes to the side and examine the girl in her periphery. The girl was talking to herself, Natasha realized, low murmurs and giggles which could be heard even over the noise of the car. She looked too clean to be homeless or crazy. Natasha decided she was drunk. None of the other passengers were looking directly at her. They stared at their books and newspapers, at the ads promising clean teeth and cheaper cell service, or, as a last resort, into vacant space assuming the glassy-eyed stare of the weary and the jaded. Even their bodies betrayed their aversion. Their legs were crossed away from her, their torsos angled gently. The whole car seemed offended, repulsed, like magnets.

But they couldn't help themselves; every now and then their eyes flicked towards the girl and then back, betraying their consciousness. The air was thick with her presence, her disorder. And with each flick, Natasha's anxiety at her own inaction disappeared, soothed and validated by the dull complacency of those around her.

It was stupid to get drunk and then get on the Metro all alone, Natasha thought. Someone must have brought her here, some friends half-drunk themselves, dragging her through the turnstiles, finding the orange line, pushing her through the sliding doors, waving goodbye, smiling, laughing. She felt sick to her stomach. Tomorrow they would call, professing their worry. They would be so glad that she hadn't been mugged or worse, because really for a few dollars anyone could get on the Metro, and with a little ill luck, anything could happen.

Stupid, Natasha thought again, and pressed her cheek against the scratched and foggy glass of the window, watching in the dark reflection as the girl spilled to the floor just as the car stopped at the next station.

A man banged his briefcase on Natasha's knee as he slipped through the doors, eager to flee. He slammed against a mass of short skirts, high heels, synthetic colours, and vulnerable flesh. The skirts laughed as he ran off, blew him a kiss, and squeezed against Natasha's bruised knee as they passed.

She lowered her eyes and ignored the new arrivals, grateful for their loud excited shrieks, their high-pitched vulgarity, which swallowed whole the low-pitched moaning of the thing still sprawled across the aisle.

Hey, one of the girls said. She had inexplicably coated all available flesh in a thick layer of body glitter. In the dark of a club, or even the dark of the street, the shimmer might have been something wonderful, a surprise as beautiful and unexpected as the flecks of glitter reflected in the pavement on moonlit nights. But in the well-lit fluorescent of the metro car, she looked downright ghoulish.

Hey, she said again. Is that girl okay?

She was looking at the drunk girl and Natasha followed her eyes to the thing on the floor, now rocking from side to side, her black hair like a torn fan, her legs scissored apart pushing her jean skirt up around her waist.

Natasha blushed.

The glitter girl had walked up to the drunk girl and was now in the process of coaxing her up. Her friends surrounded her and soon they were brushing her hair back in place, pulling her skirt back down over her thighs, asking her questions in a soothing tone.

Are you okay? Where's your stop?

Out of the slurred mouth of the drunk girl came a slow indecipherable mumble. The girls leaned forward, begged her to repeat it again.

Natasha felt the heat rise to her cheeks, raised her frozen fingers, and pressed them into the flame of her face. She stared at the plastic moulding in front of her, the curve of wall melting into window. Someone had scratched a heart deep into the Plexiglas.

A single beat of shame pulsed collectively through the car. Now the passengers were staring at their feet, feeling guilt at their previous complacency. I am not like them, Natasha thought. I am not like you, Natasha said, raising her head.

What?

The glitter girl and her friends stared at Natasha.

Saint-Henri, Natasha mumbled. She's saying her stop is Place Saint-Henri. I can take her.

And that was how Natasha found herself tangled in the embrace of a woman who reeked of alcohol, dragging her up the escalator with a sinking feeling of regret. Through sheer tenacity and a small bit of violence, Natasha wrestled her burden through the turnstiles and out of the warm, protective enclave of the Metro station.

She could feel the sharp gusts of air blowing in cool and strong off the street. For a minute she thought about the sweet relief of abandoning the girl by the ticket booth, but she pushed the thought down and began instead to shout questions at her, shaking her by the shoulders. It was useless. She had withdrawn into an alcohol-induced fugue, her eyes unfocused, lids closing.

A heavy hand touched her lightly on the back of the shoulder. Suspicious, she turned to see a tall, well-dressed man, a man with a kind face, a man old enough to be her father.

You don't know her? he asked. He spoke with the hint of an accent—a vulnerability so delicate it was disarming.

Dazed, Natasha shook her head.

It was very nice of you to bring her here. Thank you. I take her now.

His hands, firm and capable, were already moving her to the side. When he let go of her to pick up the drunk girl, cradling her against his chest like a child, she missed their solid warmth against her back.

What are you doing? Natasha asked slowly as he shifted her carefully in his arms. The girl moaned pitifully, reached up a hand to push him away, and then let it fall, too exhausted to carry through the motion.

Natasha reached forward and latched onto the girl's wrist protectively.

I'm taking her home, the man said with surprise. He tried to move forward but Natasha clung onto the drunk girl's wrist

I'm her boyfriend, he said smiling patiently.

His words carried the weight of well-worn familiarity. He seemed too old to be the drunk girl's boyfriend and yet Natasha felt herself waver towards belief under the pressure of his steady eyes.

Thank you, he repeated, beginning to walk in slow firm steps so that Natasha's grip on the girl loosened as she strove to follow.

I'm going to take her home now. Don't worry.

He turned and looked Natasha straight in the eye.

It's fine, I'm her boyfriend.

But still Natasha clung on. He refused to slow his pace so Natasha had to trot along briskly to follow. The three of them, locked together by misplaced duty and obligation, shuffled forward in a ridiculous dance, the man repeating with less patience and more exasperation that the girl in his arms was his girlfriend.

She realized suddenly that they had walked out of the Metro into the open air of the city street. It was dark and gusty, dead autumnal leaves circled each other, dancing with the wind. She felt suddenly unreasonably tired as if she had just awoken from a deep sleep. She felt very small and very alone, in the dark at night with a tall man she did not know. She wanted to go home and kick off her shoes and curl into her bed, to sleep warm and safe and cocooned, to lock the world out and forget about this man and this girl, these people who had imposed themselves on her through their own carelessness.

Let go of her wrist, he said.

She let go of the wrist.

The man smiled. He tipped his head politely towards her before he turned away, his prize cradled in his arms.

Wait, Natasha called.

But her sweet voice drowned on its way to his ears, lost in the cold sharp whistle of the wind. She thought of running after him but instead she stood where he had left her, listening to his hurried steps, watching as he walked away from her, a drunk girl in his arms.

She found herself telling the story to her girlfriends in the following weeks. Their reactions were curiously uniform. You were so kind to help her, so kind to brave that strange man in the middle of the night. I'm sure he was her boyfriend. I'm sure, I'm sure.

MOTHER

MOTHER BRUSHES MY HAIR, 100 strokes with the silver comb, each night before I go to bed. She does it while I'm sitting at my vanity, counting off strokes one at a time in that bored, flat voice of hers. Sometimes I like to watch us in the mirror as she does it, a mother and daughter engaged in a loving act of care, but tonight Mother's face is pale and angry and when she hits a tangle at the base of my neck, instead of pinching off the hair with one hand and carefully working through the tangle with the comb, she yanks the comb down, the corners of her mouth pinching upwards in a smile at my anguished shriek. After that I keep my eyes closed.

Sometimes, when Mother is obedient, I like to comb her hair out, pretend that I am the mother and she is the child. I am always careful to start at the base of her hair and work my way down, never letting the comb catch on a single knot in Mother's rich thick hair. But tonight will not be one of those nights. When Mother counts off the 100th stroke she does it with a sigh, pulling the teeth out of my hair before the stroke is well and truly done. When I open my eyes she pulls some strands of my hair from the comb and places them in the garbage bin like a real mother should.

But when I go to kiss her on the cheek and bid her good night she recoils from my lips. And when I say, Good night, Mother, as she is walking from my room, she turns around. Her eyes catch mine in the vanity mirror and as we stare at each other she says, I'm not your fucking mother.

Mother is a dreamer, her head in the clouds. This makes her an indifferent cook; sometimes the porridge turns out fine, other times I have to discreetly pick out flecks of black from the dried-out slop and try to swallow down what remains. Anything more complicated than eggs often turns out bad, the eggs are often bad as well. Father pointedly doesn't say anything when these things happen and I know it is my fault so I don't say anything either. One time, early on, she did something to the food, I'm not sure what. It made Father sick for days and Mother cried and cried like nothing else, a hopeless sort of sobbing, when she realized it wouldn't kill him. I had to cook for a while after that and it was hard, making the food for me and my older brother, Jimmy, and Father. It never tasted right to me, though the others swore it was as good as any grown woman could make. Father didn't want me to feed Mother, wanted me to starve her down, but it takes awhile to make a good and proper meal and in those hours, when it was just me and Mother in the kitchen, I couldn't help it if food from the cutting board would tumble off in her direction. At the end of the week when Father brought a bowl of cold scraps to her, her first real meal in all that time, and set it in front of her and asked her if she had learned her lesson she kept her head down so that he patted her on the head and said, Good girl, and let her eat in peace. He hadn't given her a fork and so she had to eat with her hands, biting at her own fingers in her haste to chew the food she was parcelling into her mouth. But halfway through her eyes flitted towards mine and in that fierce look she gave me I knew that she hadn't learned her lesson, quite the opposite in fact, and I had done wrong.

I was in a mood the day we found Mother. We had piled into the car together, me and Father and Jimmy, with me in the back like always. Jimmy put his window all the way down so that the gusts of wind blowing in upstream tangled my long hair and whipped it into a cage all around my face. Not that I minded. Tears were fluttering to my eyes and bile rising in my throat the whole ride. We drove for most of the day and the anger rode right along with me so that when we finally stopped for dinner, after a full day of driving and eating in the car, as Father and Jimmy tore into their burgers I found I couldn't touch my food. Couldn't conceive of the idea of hunger or of ever being hungry again.

Father didn't say anything though I know he can't abide sulking. He waited till he was done before he asked if I was going to touch my meal and when I shook my head no, knowing if I said more I would either cry or scream, he gave a nod to Jimmy, who snatched the food off my plate and ate it up in big bites. After that we got back into the car and drove.

But though Mother calls Father a monster there must be a kind of softness in him. Because the following morning when we found the place, a busy gas station–diner, he asked me if I saw anyone who looked like a mother. He had never let me pick before and I knew that was his way of saying sorry.

There are rules for how a mother should be. Father never set them down to Jimmy and me the way the rules of the house are written down, written in pencil with letters formed by his own hand on yellowed paper and taped to the fridge, but I know them anyway. A mother should be modest. A mother should be neither old nor young. A mother should be plump but not fat. A mother should be pretty but not beautiful. A mother should have a soft temperament.

All the mothers Father brought to us, even though they were different in their own ways, all of them fell within these margins, all of them blended into this lump of mother-shaped women. So I knew what it was I should be looking for.

We waited all day to see a mother. All day sitting in that car, with the windows rolled down and the sweat rolling off us, watching the entrance to the diner, women coming and going, women of all sizes and shapes, dozens that could have been a mother. Towards the end of the day Jimmy got impatient and leaned back and told me to pick someone for God's sake, and Father, rather than tweaking his ear for speaking so, the way he would have done if it were me, Father merely laid a heavy hand on the nape of Jimmy's neck, immediately quieting him. That was another unspoken rule. Finding a mother should never be rushed.

There were still people coming in and out of the diner by the time the sun set, fewer women but still some, but nevertheless at a certain point without warning us, Father turned on the ignition and we left in silence. I had never slept in a bed that was not my own before, but I spent that night in a motel where Father took out two rooms, what I thought would be one for him and one for us. When he pulled up to the doors of the room he handed me the key to one and he and Jimmy went in the other. It was my punishment to be alone I suppose but being in a room all by myself, lying in that big bed with the scratchy polyester comforter felt luxurious. There was a little soap wrapped up in pink paper in the bathroom and a toothbrush with a head wrapped in plastic and even though I knew that they must be there for my use I could barely bring myself to touch them, let alone open them.

I couldn't ever remember being by myself in that way with no Father, no Jimmy, no Mother even to watch me. And though there were sounds that bled through the walls, the engines of cars past their prime crawling down the highway, the too-loud TV of my motel neighbours, I knew that just across the way were my father and Jimmy and that even if they resented the fact that because of me we were still motherless and adrift after one day of watching, if I were truly in trouble, if I screamed out in the night, they both would be there to protect me.

I had tried to stay up as long as I could, the better to enjoy the novelty of staying in my own room, but I woke to a loud knock on the door, Father announcing that it was already morning and time to go. After a few minutes in the car I realized that we weren't going back to the diner of the previous day and I felt a bitter sickness in the pit of my stomach, the unsettling acidic feeling of failure settling over me. But here Father's generosity of spirit appeared once again. When we pulled up to a semi-abandoned parking lot at the outskirts of a small town, the weeds growing chest-high between the cracks in the asphalt, Father gave me a nod, quick and easy, his chin bobbing up and down in my direction. It was enough of a signal for both me and Jimmy who groaned loudly and then stared out the window in exaggerated indifference as if he were not terribly annoyed that Father had once again allowed me the picking.

I knew her immediately when I saw her, even if she was all wrong, even if she was not the mother that Father and Jimmy had been hoping for. She was distinct, a tall ropey lean thing, with the broad shoulders and slim hips of a man. She wore short shorts and a man's tank top, loose around the armholes so that not only could we see the pink straps of her cheap pink bra, but the sides of it too.

She had pulled up to the gas station across the way, one of a handful of customers, and we all watched her, Father and Jimmy and I, as she unfurled her long limbs from her car, stretched her hands skyward so that her tank top rode up exposing a narrow smile of flesh around her midriff. Even though she was far away I could see that she was young. It wasn't just the way she stretched herself, or the boys' clothes she wore. It was that hair of hers that reached all the way down her back. It was the hair of a girl who has only herself to think of, not the hair of a woman whose life is a long chain of chores where long hair would only be a burden to be pulled, burned, stuck. The hair was like a separate entity: it moved when she was still, it trailed with great reluctance behind her as she moved. It was the hair that made me point at her, unthinking and all feeling and say, That one.

And even though Jimmy cursed me and there was a hesitance in all of Father's movements as he turned the car engine back on and we began to trail her car as she pulled away from the gas station, unaware that we were there, her future family, following close behind, I knew that she was mine. My mother.

The problem with the young ones, Father said to no one in particular that first day, is that they don't understand their own fragility. As a person ages they become more tender. Not about the wide world or their fellow man, but about themselves.

Father knew of this tenderness but we were too young to know it yet ourselves.

We were sitting on the porch, Father and Jimmy and me and we were ignoring Mother's screams from inside that had early on taken the form of a string of demonic curse words and had lately curdled into an unending wordless groan. It was hard to listen to. Our home was small and there were only so many chores to do outside. So we sat on the porch and we tried to wait her out.

Take my hand for example.

Father presented his hand to Jimmy and me for inspection and dutifully we looked at it, ignoring the bellow that burst forth from inside the house.

Father told me to put my hand out and obligingly I did. My hand was lighter than his and taut too. The ropey veins that protruded from his knuckles to his wrists were faint underwater rivers in my hand.

Once, Father began, ignoring the wail that had risen from inside. Once I had a hand as smooth and untarnished as yours. Think of that. Your father as a young man.

He paused so that we might think on it, but all I could imagine, even if I closed my eyes, was my father's weathered face on a child's small body.

It was my job to train Mother up. Her duties were domestic in nature and since I was the only girl I knew what had to be done like the back of my hand. To make Father's bed and Jimmy's. To clean the house, dusting once a day, washing the floors once a week. And of course she was to cook for us, the most dangerous and challenging part of her work for us as well as her.

It occurred to me as I listed off the chores, reciting them quickly as her tears kept coming, that someone must have taught the chores to me. Some mother, all the mothers, had trained me in their way. And now I trained them back.

She cried in the beginning. Longer than I thought possible. More than any of the others. It was her youth, I thought, as I watched her shake and tremble as she tried to form words. With Father she was like an animal, kicking and spitting, testing the limits of her chains, but alone with me she was different, more human. She would try to calm herself, so she could have the words to plead with me. I could see she thought it was just a matter of reasoning with me, or rather of making me see what *she* called reason. She didn't like it when I called her Mother, kept begging me to call her her before name, her *real* name as she kept calling it. When I kept right on calling her Mother she switched tactics.

I know you want to think the best of your Father, she would say. But what he's doing is bad. He *hurts* me, she said.

She was so careful with her words in the beginning.

Later, when she understood that allusions had no effect on me, she started using different words, explicit ones. Father had taught me that showing anger was a form of weakness, but when Mother started telling me stories, stories of what Father did to her at night I had to put down whatever I was holding, the dishrag or a book, and walk out of the house. Had to keep walking until I was outside of her view and then I ran myself ragged, ran till I couldn't keep my breath, and still there was so much anger inside of me that I kept walking, kept walking till I found Garbage Edge, our name for the cliff near our house. So called because the cliff was where Father tossed our refuse too big to burn.

I stared down to where the trees were, far below, where they grew so thick and voluminous that they swallowed up anything that would fall down there. I imagined what it would be like to fling myself off the edge, to be swallowed up by those trees, and when I was done imagining I picked my way home. By the time I got back it was dark and Father and Jimmy were halfway through their meals. Mother got up to serve me, so docile and sweet her leg chains barely rattled. I ate that meal slow and steady but I said not one word so I finished before Father and Jimmy were done. And when I looked up I could see that though Mother looked as obedient as a dog there was a cruel look of cunning in her eyes for she knew that she had poisoned my thoughts and I would never be able to look at Father the same way again.

Things were different after that. Mother acted tame around Father and Jimmy. Housebroke, Father used to call it. She never rattled her chains, she never spoke out of turn. She was still a bad cook and a worse cleaner but she did her chores without a word of complaint. It was during the day, when it was just the two of us, that she was true. She talked to me less like a mother and more in the way I imagine a sister might be like. She told me, for example, about her life before. How she had left home and learned how to cook, not well obviously, but enough to sustain herself. That in the before she was a chemistry student and how much she loved to read books, the thicker the volume and the smaller the print the more easily she could lose herself in the words on the page. She told me about her own mother and her face looked pained when she told me these stories but she shared them anyway, about how her mother was a fool for love, chasing one man after another, broken-hearted after each relationship eventually ended. And she wanted to know about me too. About what life was like with Father and Jimmy. About where our mother was. When I told her she was our mother she wanted to know about our true mother and then she had to explain . . . well, explain the way that children come into this world, something I couldn't quite believe when she told me and was too embarrassed to ask Father to confirm.

It was perhaps something about the look on her face when she talked about her own mother and the string of successive men in her life that made me tell her about all the mothers I had known. It was hard to explain to her, for every mother had only that one name in common, but they were all so different and as I spoke I could recall each one, so that I spoke of Mother with the skewed nose, and Mother with the kind voice, and Mother who pinched.

But what happened to the mothers? she finally asked me, and I shrugged like we both didn't know, but I could tell from the way her voice trembled that she already did.

When I was younger and more heartless it didn't seem to matter what kind of mother I had. But the last one. Oh the last one. She had been kind from the beginning. If she cried or if she shouted it happened so early on that I couldn't remember it. What I do remember was the way she used to pull me onto her lap, cradling me against the warm soft expanse of her. I never had toys the way she explained other children had toys. But she used to fold the dust cloths in such a way that they had vague forms and sit me on her lap and do the voices. She never asked me for a thing, not once. But I began to want to do things for her and that was when the trouble began.

I don't remember exactly how or when I discovered it, but I always knew that Father kept the key to the leg chain pressed between the pages of a book on joinery. And the more I grew to care for the last mother the more I thought of that key, tucked between the pages, screaming into my thoughts, sneaking into my dreams.

I didn't mean to do it but one day, when Father and Jimmy were going to be gone all day into town to pick up some of what we needed, I let Mother go free. Just as soon as I heard the truck pull away I went to the joinery book and shook loose the key and as the last mother watched I undid her chains.

She ran her hands through my hair so tenderly after I did it and then walked out of the house.

That was the last time I saw her.

I thought when Father and Jimmy came home there would be hell to pay, but when they came home it seemed that Mother had already paid it. Of course I was still beaten within an inch of my life, a backhand from Father that left a hand-shaped bruise on my face and then whipped across my bottom till it was raw and bleeding but that wasn't the worst. The worst was when Jimmy told me that the last mother was with the rest of them, thrown into the pit of trees off Garbage Edge.

I tell Mother this and I don't even realize I'm crying till she's thumbing a tear off my face. I'm telling her this because Jimmy and Father don't understand but also because I like her, because more than anything I need her to be fearful so that she'll stay alive. But she doesn't look afraid.

Delilah, she says, using my real name instead of calling me Daughter because she's disobedient, because she thinks real names will save her.

Delilah, I can help you. Let me go like you let the last one go. Save me and I'll save you. You're a kid. No one will blame you.

I can't, I say because it's true.

How long do you think this will go on? she asks me. A man like your father . . . what do you think they're going to do to you when you get older?

I don't know what to say to that. I like being a daughter, being here with Jimmy and Father and the mothers. I've never wanted to grow up.

Daddy, I say, the word feeling strange and unfamiliar in my mouth. We are a formal family and Daddy is such a little girl word. But I want Father to think of me as a little girl and when he turns to me with a smile I know that my ploy has worked.

What do you think I'll be when I grow up?

His face darkens immediately.

Has your mother been putting thoughts in your head?

I shake my head quickly.

I mean do you think I'll be a good wife someday? A good mother?

The clouds clear and his smile is back.

The very best.

Dinner is roast chicken with potatoes and root vegetables and it is good because I made it and unlike Mother I am good-tempered and have a willingness to please and improve.

Father says it is delicious and even though Jimmy has to be pushed into agreeing he eventually does with an ungrateful grunt.

And how does it taste to you, Ana?

Three letters and two syllables that change the mood around the table completely.

I love it, Ana says.

She smiles at me and I smile back, two women sharing a moment of joy across the men's discomfort.

Ana, whom I love.

Ana, who is not my mother.

Ana, who by tomorrow will be in the pit at the bottom of Garbage Edge.

A CHANGE OF ATMOSPHERICS

HE'S JUST SOMEONE ELSE'S boyfriend, sidling up to her at a bar, trying to convince her that no really, his girlfriend doesn't mind a quick flirt with another woman. She doesn't even try to stop her eyes from rolling.

If you were mine, she tells him, I'd kill any girl who tried to flirt with you. No, scratch that, she says off his smirk, I'd kill *you*.

He's still grinning, under the mistaken assumption that what she's said is cute, that it has something to do with how great he is instead of how batshit she is.

Everything in the bar is blue: the lights, his eyes, her mood. Her drink is the toxic aqua of cleaner fluid. She drains it and orders another. She wonders if she has the money to pay for it. It doesn't matter really. He's the type of guy who would pay with a smile, who wouldn't expect anything in return (who would still try to get a little something).

While he talks she stares at her arm trying to gauge its actual colour. It should be a light brown, but instead it's stained blue just like everything else. Difficult to tell whether it's blue-filtered light or she's stumbled into a blue-scale world. That sort of thing has happened before. A world of greyscale where everyone spoke German for some reason or for no reason at all. His name had been Dieter or Dietrich then and his eyes had been various shades of dark.

What a pity you can't see colour, she had told him that time after she had told him her name but before she had kissed him.

What's colour? he had asked.

It feels like forever since that kiss in black and white. She sips her drink and tries to remember when forever was. Last year? Last Tuesday? She doesn't know the difference anymore.

In the blue bar she interrupts whatever inanity is coming out of his mouth with a question.

I know my name, she says, but what's yours?

Valentine, he says.

Valentine, she repeats. It suits him, suits how pretty he is, how wide-eyed. Everything about him, from his slouch to his eager eyes, so easy. She wishes she smoked so she could stub the cigarette out on his arm, make him feel burned and scared for the first time in this life. She wants him to know the painful cost of surprise. Then, just as quickly, she feels ashamed of her own thoughts.

What did you say? she asks without interest, ducking her head forward and mumbling into her drink, trying to clear her head.

I said, I told you mine, now you tell me yours.

She feels herself softening unexpectedly.

Oh, sweetheart, she says. That's the one thing that always stays the same.

He never remembers her; she never stops hoping he will.

There are only three things that never change: her desire for him, her own self, and Ms. Gutiérrez. Even her parents disappear from time to time only to reappear in increasingly wild variations. She's not sure she really has parents anymore. The last time she saw them was the time they were both dogs.

It was wonderful, she explained to Ms. Gutiérrez. I took them out for walks and patted them on the head and gave them treats.

And me, Ms. Gutiérrez asked. I was a dog too?

No, I told you. You stay the same no matter what. They were dogs and on Wednesday I came here and sat on the couch as usual and I told you I was concerned I would turn into a dog too.

And?

And you said you didn't think it would happen, but you gave me a dog biscuit just in case.

Ms. Gutiérrez laughed at that.

In the bar she's switched from the cleaner fluid to something icy and opaque. She feels warm and bubbly; if she stood up right this instant she would tremble to the ground. She and Valentine are playing a game. It's not complex really. He keeps trying to learn her name and she keeps evading his questions. His strategy mostly involves buying her drinks till she's tumble-down drunk hoping to trip her up.

She asks him, words slurring, if he's happy here. It comes out all smushed up—*reallytrulyhappy*, the words colliding against each other. He says that he's ecstatic and for a moment she believes him. Then she tells herself that he isn't really paying attention. It wasn't a fair answer. She smiles at him and hopes he doesn't notice how her eyes are tearing up, how she is distracted thinking of all the things in this life that might make him happy, thinking about that girlfriend he mentioned earlier who doesn't mind.

Something is bothering her and so she taps Valentine on the shoulder to get his attention even though he's looking straight at her.

I have a question for you.

And I have one for you.

Do you know what colour is? Green, orange, ultraviolet?

He hesitates and she can't tell if it's because the question is absurdly obvious or completely unheard of.

You tell me what your name is and then I'll tell you if I know what colour is.

Io, she says and letting go feels like such a relief she wonders why she didn't do it before. My name is Io.

He smiles and for an instant she lets herself believe that there is recognition in his look. That he sees who she is.

He flicks her on the nose.

Of course I know what colour is, dummy.

Outside is damp and she can't remember if it was like that before she got there. She notes with satisfaction that he is right: there are colours other than blue in this world. The pavement glitters grey under her shoes.

She knows she is drunk because she keeps repeating over and over again, You have two feet, you have two feet, but sometimes you have four.

Ms. Gutiérrez would say that this was self-medicating, but then again Ms. Gutiérrez isn't here, might not even exist, won't for certain until Wednesday whenever that might be. One time she was lost in a world with no Wednesdays and she thought she would never see Ms. Gutiérrez again.

The problem, she thinks as she looks down, is not whether he has two feet or four, but that she can't feel any of the feet she has. She stumbles and Valentine puts an arm around her waist, half hauling her upwards, half keeping her in a straight line.

One time you were the letter O, she says stroking his face fondly. I curled up inside you and made you whole.

Uh-huh.

He is too busy concentrating on keeping her upright to pay attention to what she is saying.

Hey, she says, trying to get him to slow down, to pay attention, to remember something, anything of who she is. She wants to tell him how hard it is to keep finding him like this, completely ignorant of who or what she is. How it hurts every time she makes him fall in love with her again. Everything she wants to say sounds like an accusation so she settles on a question she doesn't want to ask.

What's your girlfriend like?

He can't look her in the eye. He's blushing now, a warm romantic petal on his cheeks. She is so glad they are out of that blue bar, out of that blue room, so that she can stand here in his arms and watch the petal blossom.

My girlfriend is an angel, he says at last and while her heart breaks a part of her wonders if he means that literally.

Ms. Gutiérrez said that if (if!) what Io was saying was true, then there were probably only a finite amount of worlds she could go to.

So it might stop one day?

Given the amount of variation between one world and the next—it's possible that the difference between one world and the other is a nanosecond of difference, between when an eyelash falls and when it doesn't.

Io stared at her.

What I'm saying, Ms. Gutiérrez said, is that given the span of the average human life, the amount of time you spend in each place, and the possible amount of difference between one place and the next, that finite might as well be infinite. What I'm saying is that it won't stop, not until you let me help you.

Io knew that help meant little blue capsules in orange plastic bottles. Help meant a papery taste on the tongue that would be swallowed with water. Help meant no more Dieter, no more Valentine.

She didn't know if she wanted that kind of help.

He doesn't want to talk about his girlfriend, so of course it's the only thing she wants to talk about. She wants the girlfriend laid out, ugly and bare, under the floodlight of her questions. He reluctantly answers everything she asks, and she knows he thinks it is because she is stubborn and drunk, but really she knows it is because she is Io and he is hers even when he has a different name, even when he can't remember her, even when he thinks he belongs to some other woman.

Does she look like me? Io asks and juts her chin out a little to a more flattering angle.

No, he says.

And how do we compare?

You're all dark to her light. Night to her day. Her skin is pale and yours is dark as . . .

He trails off and circles her wrist with his hand so that she feels like maybe she's the possession.

It's a feeling she could get used to.

One time they found each other and it was perfect. His name wasn't Valentine then and his eyes were a different colour, but she knew him immediately and he knew her. If she was ever going to stop it at all she might have stopped it then; she could have stopped it then, but she didn't and he died, unhappy and sick and full of pain. Or so she heard. She wasn't there to see it. When it happened she was walking down streets that were too familiar hoping that there would be a change and she would be somewhere else, somewhere better. Of course it didn't happen then, right when she wanted it to. She didn't get to leave that place for a long, long time. When she finally did and she found him again it wasn't the same, she couldn't bring herself to touch him, to love him when he couldn't remember her. She thought that maybe the next change would make her whole again. Or maybe the next change. Or maybe the next.

She would like you, Valentine says, and it ruins whatever moment they were having. The two of you, and me, we could get along very well.

He leans in close.

I want to see you both, he breathes into her ear, moving against each other, light against dark.

She pushes him away from her, annoyed, not caring if she falls flat on her face or not. This is not the way it is supposed to be. It should be Io and Valentine, not Io, Valentine, and Valentine's girlfriend. There is something not quite right in his tone, something that is telling her that he is seeing her in a way she does not want to be seen. Seeing only one thing and not all the others. She stumbles away and he follows at a distance. He's always been able to read her well. He won't try again.

Every now and then Ms. Gutiérrez gives her new pills to replace the ones which she does not take. She keeps them on her though. They are in her pocket whenever she has a pocket to keep them in.

If you want it to stop, Ms. Gutiérrez says, you have to start taking them.

Once you were an edifice, Io tells Valentine as he trails behind her. Do you have any idea how easy it is to fall in love with a bevelled edge?

Not that easy as it had turned out. Not that gratifying to love something that could not bend to love you back.

He doesn't say anything and she begins to think he's ignoring her until he pipes up as they turn a corner, his words almost lost in the rush of a car slipping by.

It's called objectophilia.

And maybe she loves him a little bit for knowing that word.

Are you happy? she asks.

This time he is serious to match her seriousness. He looks in her eyes, up at the moon, down at her feet, wondering, considering a life that he's lived and has been living away from and apart from her.

She reaches into her pocket while she's waiting for his answer and finds the pill bottle where she knew it would be. With her thumb she pops the cap, feels the cool little capsules slide into the lint-filled crevices and traces the shape of one repeatedly with her fingertips. All she needs to do to stay here is take one. And then another one. And then another. She could stop the world from changing one day at a time. All he has to do is say one word.

Yeah, he says, his boyish grin so earnest that she feels something breaking within her in response.

Yeah, what?

She needs him to say it aloud. If he says it aloud, she thinks, then she'll find the courage to do what she has to do.

I'm happy.

Then what do you want me for?

There is more bitterness in the words than she expected to be there, but he doesn't notice or pretends not to.

Happiness on top of happiness. Happiness squared, he singsongs too close now, one hand in her hair.

She knows what she's supposed to do. Push him away with one hand and with the other pinch the pill between her fingers and swallow it. Without the aid of water it'll burn her mouth. She'll feel its every movement as it slides down her throat, an unwelcome invader. And it will all be worth it because he's happy. And if he's happy so is she.

Instead she closes her eyes and leans forward. In the instant before they kiss both their eyes flicker open and she sees that his aren't really blue after all. Then she presses her lids shut and she feels his lips brushing against her own.

It is biting cold when she opens her eyes. She is all alone on a different street in a different city in a different world and wherever she is it must be Wednesday for she can already feel a pull leading her to wherever Ms. Gutiérrez might be.

COMMON ANIMALS

THE FIRST TIME HE turned into a wolf it was chill and it was February and we were fighting about something. I can't remember what it was exactly we were fighting about, but it seemed important at the time, the way things do before they're completely and utterly dwarfed by your significant other metamorphosing from human to beast. One minute he was there, his face distorted, jaw unhinged, and then he was simply not, replaced instead with this angry, hairy, violent *thing*.

It's your fault had been the last thing he said before he turned, veins bulging from his forehead. It's your fault. Flecks of his spittle landed delicately on my wrist. The echoes of that missive ran round and round my head as I stared at its snout, its snapping jaws. Well, I thought blankly, now you've done it.

Its teeth were large and jagged and its pink tongue kept rolling obscenely over them, sending off thick white flecks of foam. I could feel this new kind of wet leaking hungrily onto my arms and it sent licks of revulsion over my body. I kept my eyes trained on its mouth, its big sharp teeth. As if by staring I could reverse the process and make it go from beast to man again. And then it lunged at me and a wave of terror plunged me down so that my legs sank under me and I poured onto the ground.

I'm going to die, I thought. I closed my eyes so I wouldn't have to watch it happen and I felt a kind of calming gladness. Soon it would all be over and I wouldn't have to try to rationalize or understand the absurdity. I would die and there would be a clean end to it.

But, of course, I didn't and there wasn't.

When I opened my eyes I was screaming and there was a warm choking mass on top of me, but I was still alive and unharmed. There was a small space inside me, an inch by an inch thick maybe, a little box inside my brain, and from that tiny space I felt I was watching all of this unfold with a calm and tired certainty. Stop screaming, I told my body from inside this box. Stop making a fuss.

What had happened, I could see now, was that I had slid down when the wolf jumped forward allowing the brunt of its force to hit the wall. There was a soft depression there now. It didn't seem like the force that caused that dent would be force enough to stop the wolf, but it had and the wolf was now unconscious and on top of me, the furry density of it crushing the breath out of me. I took both hands and pressed them against the warm breathing side of the thing and felt its ribs push back under the skin. Another push and then another and finally it rolled off my body and I was free to stand on legs as unsteady as those of a newborn calf.

I don't know how I got out of the apartment, how I managed to work the locks to make the door open. I must have though because I did get out. The last thing I remember before stepping out into the hallway was looking back, just the once. The wolf was crumpled up like a collection of ratty fur coats heaped carelessly on the floor. And then there was a flicker. Those heavy lids struggling to wake. That was the moment I turned and ran. Even in my panic, all I could think about was how, when its eyes opened, he seemed not at all wolflike but very much like a human wearing a wolf suit.

It wasn't till I made my way down to the lobby that I realized I had no shoes on and it was deep winter, one of those rare, pretty Ottawa evenings when the snow is flying flake-thick as if someone had shaken up a snow globe. I didn't know what to do. I didn't have any friends in the building even though we had lived there for nearly two years. He had always said that the people there were not worth knowing, that they were ignorant or arrogant or not quite right in some undefinable way, though I never quite understood what he meant. The other tenants seemed fine to me, polite and friendly in the indifferent way of strangers. Now and again, one or the other of them caught my eye and I felt a faint yearning for friendship. Still, I had not thought it worthwhile to pursue anything further. I would have never been able to invite any of them into our home; he sulked through any social occasion he did not initiate, refusing to say a word. He rebuffed each effort to engage him, only increasing the discomfort. It would have been embarrassing both for me and for the friend I longed to acquire. So I hadn't tried, not for a long time.

I knew a few people in the city, co-workers and a couple of acquaintances, but I couldn't imagine how I could reach them or, having done so, how to explain what had happened. The event was too fantastical to be believed.

So I spent the night crouched in the stairwell, shivering and hoping no one would find me and force me to explain myself. As I counted down the hours I thought of the day we had moved in together, of the solidness of unpacking boxes and commingling our books. In the kitchen we had found that we had two sets of everything. I thought it was a sign when I discovered we had twin blenders, purchased on the cheap from the same grocery store before we even knew each other.

In the months that followed we slowly combed through everything together, optimistically purging all of our doubles. He kissed my hand each time I finally let go of one of our redundancies. It occurred to me now that almost all the somethings we discarded had been mine.

I woke up, my body uncurling painfully as if covered by a giant bruise. I could hear the mechanical whir of the elevator and realized that it was morning and I wasn't dead after all, and if I wasn't dead then I should probably get ready for work. So I let my feet guide me to my apartment door, which was closed but mercifully unlocked, and went in. It was not worth thinking about what I was doing and why I was doing it. It was enough that I was home.

He was there, him, not the wolf, making breakfast, preparing to go to work. I sat down and watched him make it, watched him eat it, watched him scrape the excess into the garbage without asking me if I wanted any, without talking to me, without looking at me at all. Bye, I said as I watched him walk out the door. If he heard me he did not acknowledge it.

I got ready for work and as I brushed my teeth I searched myself in the mirror for signs of what had happened. But as I examined first one cheek and then the other, as I inspected my arms and legs, I found there were no bruises, no scratches, no evidence at all that I had tangled with a wolf and lived. I could almost allow myself to believe that nothing had happened at all. Almost. Before I left, I touched the dent in the wall.

I don't remember the second time he turned into a wolf.

I don't remember the third.

What I do remember are the worst times, the times when I fought back. He began to turn more and more often, clawing at my clothes, stalking me like prey around the apartment, one attack bleeding into the next. I dodged them as best I could, spent many sleepless hours cowering in the stairwell or walking around the block, hoping that by the time I came back it would be gone and he would be back. But when I fought back things devolved. Sometimes to keep the bites at bay I would hit him with whatever was at hand. A broom. A cup. One time an ashtray. I hurled it so near his head that the shattered glass shards embedded themselves in his skin and made blood run through the fur. I watched him whimper, saw the hurt in his eyes. I felt the resistance die inside me even as he rallied and came back again, twice as hard.

Our home became full of broken things. Our bedroom door splintered, a safety deposit I'd never get back. The lock on the bathroom door smashed. Our double French doors missing panes for reasons I don't care to remember. And then of course all the dents in the walls. The one from the first time and then the others. Ones that he made. Ones that I made.

For a long, long time I thought it was as bad as it was ever going to get. I kept my head down and tried to avoid the bites. I even believed I had a small measure of control. That I could provoke the wolf out of him, aggravate him if I needed to, and rid myself of the tension of wondering when the next time would be. I thought that if nothing else I was good at this one thing. Then, one day, it was my time to grow angry.

There was a lamp I owned with a green glass base, a gift from my mother. This one day, when I failed to pay adequate attention to him as he was talking, he pawed it from my bedside table. If it had fallen any other way it might have rolled away unscathed or simply cracked into manageable pieces. But somehow it fell wrong, exploded magnificently. He looked a little apologetic afterwards as if he couldn't quite believe what had happened, hadn't meant to push things so far. It was that look of remorse that ate me up from the inside out, till I was more rage than anything else. He had broken so many things of mine by this time, I wouldn't have thought one more would matter. But it did. He hadn't even been the wolf when he had done it.

This time when he came at me I went back at him without pity. We fought and he bit at my wrist, his teeth cutting jaggedly into my flesh. I bit at him just as wild, tufts of fur choking my mouth. He clawed at me and I dodged his attack with an animal quickness, before turning back so I could retaliate. When I swiped at him my talons raked through fur to the soft flesh underneath. Blood beaded to the surface like rubies. I was surprised that I could do that. That I could hurt like that. When he whimpered I backed off, dropping to the ground on all fours, and limped to a corner to lick my wounds. When I lifted my wrists to assess the damage I saw that it was worse than I realized. There were no bruises or scratches, no scars. Just a thick wall of fur where my own smooth skin should have been. Where my hands had once been there were now two furry paws.

Do you see, he said laughing when it was over, when I was back to my woman shape once again. Now it's both of us.

If I ever thought of leaving that thought is long gone. How could I ever leave knowing of the slow-acting poison that lives inside me? How could I ever risk doing this to someone else? No, we will stay together.

We will be like other people: buy a house we can't afford and work jobs we are indifferent to and give up our dreams and pretend that it isn't killing us inside. When the time is right we will have little children, a boy and a girl maybe, that turn into furry werepups when the moon is full. They will nip and bite and fight. And they will know no different.

MAPS OF THE UNKNOWN

SHE LOVED HIM TO DISTRACTION.

She wanted to bite his toes, knuckles, nip at the soft skin on his upper arms, suck out his eyeballs and feel them circling in her mouth, cradled by her tongue, caged in by her teeth.

She wanted to plunge her hand deep into his chest, feel it sink past the skin and muscle and sinew and bones until the palm of her hand rested on his gently pulsing heart.

She wanted to know where he had been September third, *1943*, and what he had been thinking.

Nineteen forty-three? he asked. *Nineteen forty-three?* I wasn't *alive* in *1943*.

Okay. So where had his parents been in 1943, what had his mother been doing as she carried within her the one egg out of two million that would eventually be fertilized and gestate for nine months and then live for twenty-six years and then fall in love and then be in this bed right here, right now, with someone who loved him to distraction, wanted to tear him into tiny pieces, pick him apart atom by atom so she could keep him safe with her here forever?

Jesus, he said. I have no idea.

She wanted to know everything. First kiss, first love yes. But also: first smell, first dream, first sexually induced sneeze.

What? he asked.

She explained.

Huh, he said. I didn't know people did that. Weird.

For her he tried to go back and find all the girls that he had loved or crushed on when he was still young enough to suck his thumb. It was the ones that he could remember, the ones that he had spent the most time with, that she was least interested in.

She was like an archaeologist dusting away at the sand of the past, reconstructing bits of his life from memories, other people's memories, to be cross-referenced and indexed. She wanted to know every half-forgotten brushing of the fingertips so she could examine it from this angle or that, calculate its weight and height, classify it by its moment in time, and then file it away in a drawer robbed of any sentiment. She thought when she was done she would have a map of him, a tattered map full of holes yes, but filled with things his own forgetful mind could not recall. She would know him better than anyone else.

His first love was dead and had been for two years. A car accident had jetted her through a windshield, her skull and the glass window cracking each other irreparably. All that knowledge, all those memories, lost forever six feet underground, carried off one by one by beetles and maggots and worms. Impossible to reassemble. She mourned them.

There were things he wasn't telling her.

I tell you everything, he said.

She was sitting on a chair in the kitchen, her spine preternaturally straight, not even resting on the back of the chair. Her lips were pressed tight together in a crooked little line; she was angry.

How can you say that? she asked. You can't even tell me how many times you yawned today or if your heart skipped a beat or if you missed a breath. You don't know the first thing about yourself. You forget. I can't even trust you because you forget things you don't even mean to hide.

She could not get over this dead love. It corrupted her thoughts. How many others had there been? Strangers passed in the street, homes walked by where some head turned to the window had captured him for a moment. So many glances and acknowledgements between him and the dead, fragments which could never be recovered. But her fixation on them was all pretense; they both knew there was only one among the dead who mattered and so she returned to the dead love again and again. She asked him so many questions that by the end she could reconstruct their first meeting together as if she had been at that lacklustre dinner when they had both been with other people, as if she were the one who had shaken his hand not knowing that this was the start of everything, as if it had been her mouth offering the noncommittal word-exhale hybrid Hey that would start it all.

There were parts of him that were dead.

Is that what worries you?

Her face was buried in her arms so that her eyes could shut out the world, but her ears, her treacherous ears, were still listening to the thrum of the fridge, to the sounds of the TV leaking through the ceiling, to his every step as he walked around her.

His chair scraped against the wood floor when he sat down.

Here I am, he said.

A kiss buried in her hair.

And here.

A finger on her spine.

And here.

And he was tickling her ribs and she was laughing involuntarily through her anger and then giving in and genuinely laughing with him, laughing till there were tears in her eyes and no breath left to be angry with.

Which was why it was so confusing when he really was dead, all those years later, and kept appearing in her sleep, reassuring her the way he had in the kitchen, that he was still there.

In her Technicolor dreams they were both young and immortal and gifted with perfect memories. The map of his life was complete down to the last blink and she could fold it up and slip it in her pocket.

You thought I died? he'd say and then he would tickle her till she laughed, till she woke up crying.

Of course he had gone first, she knew that had to be the way. She had watched him over the years as his hair fell out in little piles, the smooth dome of his scalp new territory for her to explore. Wrinkles formed, disappeared, and then came back to stay, deep sunbursts fanning out from around his eyes. And then she watched as he expired, one horrible last breath that was almost too much to record. She waited for her own self to collapse after him and follow wherever he was going. But her body betrayed her. She persisted in living.

She turned him into ashes and refused to scatter him. She bided her time patiently, reading in a corner, until a thought began to wriggle in her mind as uncomfortable as a loosening tooth.

She began to wonder if souls could live on forever. Could desire outlast all rules of time and space? Had that first long-dead love been waiting all this time for the moment when her last lover would return to her, when they could find each other and be together at last, untouchable as stars?

It took effort to find the cemetery and then the grave, the marker she sought out, one among many. She had planned to go there and dig, smash through rotted wood to find rotted bone and then destroy and scatter. But by the time she found what she was looking for she was too exhausted to do anything but scrape at the grass a little with her shoe. She sat down on the base of the headstone, not even caring that it was covered in green mould. After a while she reached into her purse and pulled out the cylindrical urn that she carried with her everywhere. It took all she had left to unscrew the cap, but to tip the jar over and watch the ashes pour out, that was ease itself. When it was finally empty there was a large pile at her feet, a pile that the four winds began to sweep away, through the grass and beyond.

THE GIRL WHO CRIED DIAMONDS

ONCE THERE WAS A girl who cried diamonds, who bled rubies, who pissed gold, and who shat onyx.

The Girl was born in a tiny pueblo, an ancient place sheltered so deep among the hills and surrounded by long stretches of desert as to seem foreign to those who lived in the cities. Still, forgotten as that place was, ignored as it was, unloved as it was, to the people who were born to that corner of the Earth the land was beloved to them and held a special significance. It was considered a holy place, a sainted place. No wonder then that when the Girl was born and cried her first tears, tears that turned to diamonds smaller than dried, brittle lentils, she was regarded with only brief curiosity, before the people went back to the business of living.

The Girl was known by all in her pueblo, not because she was different, but because there were so few souls inhabiting that holy spot that those who were there knew each other as intimately as family. The people in the surrounding pueblos knew of her too, by name if not by face, and those in the pueblos surrounding *those* knew of her as well, by reputation if not by name. The further away word of her travelled, the more diluted became the story of her that was told. In this way the story of the Girl and the precious stones her body secreted were for a while kept safe from greedy minds by the cynical hearts of those who dismissed these stories as legend, fever dreams, and fantasy.

Shortly after the birth of the Girl a man who had been there to see her first tears finally gave up hope that life in the pueblo would ever change. He went to seek his fortune in the vast city which succeeded only in crushing what little hope he had left in life with degrading, ill-paid work. Drinking heavily one night years later, he told anyone who would listen about the little girl who cried diamonds when she was hungry and bled rubies when she skinned her knees. After years of living in the city he now knew the value of such things and he longed to reach back in time and take one fat tear off the child's cheek, skim the crystals from her knee, and live life as a rich man, or at least a man who could afford a few luxuries beyond the night of drinking that followed each successive payday.

Is that so? another man in the bar said to the first, tired man beside him.

The tired man had hands so thick with calluses that they were impenetrable even by the needles of a cactus, a feature that no longer was useful now that he lived in the city and all the nopales he ate were cleaned by someone else's hands.

The man he was talking to in the bar had fair skin burned pink in the sun like a pig's. He wore a suit all in white and his hands were soft and speckled with old age and thick with veins. The white man made a gesture to the barmaid to cut off the drinks of the tired man beside him believing that it was all the liquor in his blood that made him talk of little girls out of fairy tales with diamonds for tears.

And so no one believed the story and the Girl was safe.

Far away the girl who cried diamonds grew up in her pueblo and cooked food, like the others, and watched her younger siblings, like the others, and prayed to the Virgin, like the others, and grew into a small and serious young woman. Around her the pueblo grew and not so far away, but far away enough that it was almost like another world altogether, the cities swelled.

And then the growing of the pueblo stopped. Like a river suddenly choosing to reverse its course people began to leave. First the men and later the women chasing after them, leaving behind their children in search of money or their husbands. First they went to the cities and then they went farther, crossing the border into one country and sometimes going even further and crossing yet another border further north.

They sent back money, enough money to build big empty houses which they could not return to and would never see with their own eyes. Soon there were ghost houses all around the pueblo, each one bigger than the last, empty houses made of cement with several floors and a pool and large gates to keep the people who lived in the pueblo from enjoying whatever was inside.

On the way to school the children of the village would press their faces against the gates and stare through the pickets at the large houses which they did not have the right to live in or touch but which they were allowed to look at and crave.

They looked until they could stand it no more and some of them stopped looking and became habituated to simply letting their gazes drift over the empty houses, taking no more notice of them than if it had been a hill or a tree.

Some of the braver younger children, mostly boys, would break into the houses under the cover of night and see how the houses were dusty with neglect and weeds grew right up through the cement floors, life pushing through.

The pueblo began to grow sick. Men from far away came. They came in trucks and asked for the healthiest and the strongest of the men of the pueblo and those men were taken away, far away to foreign fields, to work the land in heat so hot and conditions so poor that no one of that country would take on that labour themselves. When the country turned cold they were sent back, and when the seasons changed again and the world grew hot once more they returned to work the fields. And every year fewer and fewer found their way home to the pueblo, and every year more empty houses grew in their place, like mausoleums, each one a reminder of a person or a family who had left to make a life elsewhere and would never return.

So the pueblo weakened with only the very old and the very young left to make a life there.

There came a time when the Girl's younger brother decided to leave. He was not quite a man and he was afraid to go off to lands which had swallowed his friends and neighbours whole, but he saw which way the wind was blowing and he saw that there was nothing left for him inside the pueblo. The next time he heard that a truck had come to town, looking to fill its body with the bodies of healthy young workers, he went to it. He was trailed by his sister, the girl who cried diamonds, who felt as though he were going to his death. She walked beside him on their way to the truck, never speaking to her brother, never reaching out for the small comfort of feeling his hands in hers, but the whole time feeling as though something was breaking deep inside her. When they arrived in the zócalo where the truck was ready and waiting she watched as her brother climbed aboard without looking at her once. He was one of the first, and she suffered the humiliation of standing beside the truck desperate to cling on to the scraps of a brother who was already gone in spirit, if not in body, as the truck waited for more mortals to come and feed its great belly.

At last, when the truck was nearly full, the Girl felt herself begin to cry, her tears crystallizing as they rolled down her face, the hot stones rolling to the cobblestones and splashing with a clink-clink to the ground.

The men in the truck, born of that earth, raised with that girl, held their heads high and ignored her tears, but the man driving the truck, a man born in a much bigger village a few hours away, a man who lived and worked in the city now, watched the Girl cry with astonishment.

Little one, he said in his most soothing tones. He came by her and patted her on her dark hair, stroked her rounded cheek. Why are you crying?

And the Girl explained about her brother and about the grief in her heart.

The man in the truck pretended to think on this and finally said, Dear girl. There is no reason why you should not come with us. There is opportunity enough in the city and you would be near to your brother always.

That was how the Girl found herself in the passenger seat of the truck, a place the man normally reserved for the cooler which held his drink. Drink he never offered to any of the men he ferried but which he now tenderly offered to the Girl who sat beside him.

Jostled to and fro on their way to the city, the man asked the Girl many questions about herself.

The Girl told him all about her life and her family. Her parents had left long ago for bigger cities in a strange country and had broken apart and then created other families, branches of the family tree with whom she shared blood but whom she had never met and had long ago given up hope of ever meeting.

She explained that in this country that she loved so much all she had left were little siblings who clutched at her as if she were their mother and created more work for her than if she were actually a mother herself. The only person she truly cared for was her brother in the back of the truck whom she loved dearly and who loved her dearly in turn.

Though the man in the truck pretended to listen the Girl began to suspect he was not really hearing her at all. Every time she spoke about her family he would wait for a gap in the conversation and then gently he would ask questions about her tears and how they fell and how often. She was a respectful girl and she answered all his questions honestly, wondering why he was so careful to talk in circles, never outright asking what he wanted to know but in his own clumsy way trying to get her to divine what he wanted.

In this way the time passed quickly. As they drove the winding road from pueblo to city, the life she had always known, filled with chickens and goats and half-built cinderblock homes, gave way to cars crammed with more people than she had ever seen at one time and buildings so high she had to lean back to see them.

To the Girl everything had the surreal edge of fantasy come to life. These were things she had glimpsed before, between the lines of static on a broken old TV and on the pages of a magazine, abandoned in a field where someone's visiting cousin had left it. Yet here it was now, the only thing between her and that life the dusty cracked windshield of the truck she was in.

At last the truck came shuddering to a stop beside a plain grey building that looked to the Girl like many of the other buildings they had already passed. The man driving the truck jumped out of the cab of the truck and spoke some words and the men inside the bed of the truck poured out and then poured themselves into another truck to be taken even farther away. The Girl watched as her brother disappeared and though at any moment she believed he would turn back and come to her, or at least turn back and look her in the eye, the last she saw of him was his back with the thin blades of his determined shoulders pressing against the worn pink of his cotton polo. Perhaps she was already gone to him.

She was crying when the man in the truck drove them away and did not stop even when he stopped in front of another building, similar to the first, and took her by the hand and led her to a small apartment, a place with an iron gate over a flimsy wooden door and deadbolts on both. Inside he chained her to the railing of a window and left her there with a bucket for her tears and a bucket for her refuse. These he collected daily, for daily there was such a profusion of precious stone and metal that flowed from her that he believed he would quickly become a rich man.

The man in the truck took these buckets to the only man he knew who could turn stones into paper without asking too many questions, a second-rate jeweller, a cautious man who knew his place. The first week the jeweller accepted the buckets with only a raised eyebrow. The second week he protested that he could not turn unmarked stones into coin so quickly. He wanted to know where the stones had come from and refused to assume any further risk until he could be assured that their true and rightful owners would not come to him looking for retribution.

It only took a little bit of convincing before the man with the truck brought the jeweller to the apartment where he kept the Girl, bound and gagged. He allowed him to watch the strange alchemy of her body as she pissed herself in fear of the jeweller, a warm molten gold that puddled from between her legs onto the floor and soon cooled into a disc that was easy to pick up and touch with the fingers.

Rather than express any astonishment or fear the jeweller merely congratulated the man with the truck on his conquest and went his own way. But later that night the man with the truck was murdered and the men who carried out the deed retrieved the Girl and brought her, still bound and gagged, to the home of a very rich man with whom the jeweller occasionally had business.

This rich man had a large, comfortable home and here for a brief time the girl was treated with a few small comforts. She was given a bed and fed very well with food from the rich man's own table and she was tethered by only a thin metal chain that was kept around her ankle and which she could forget about for minutes at a time if she stayed very still. The rich man had a wife and daughters and they would look at the girl who cried diamonds with pitying eyes and would sometimes beg for her to be let out and played with and would, when their father told them no, pat the Girl's hair and braid it and read to her from books. Once, when she was bored, the younger of the daughters pinched the Girl very hard on the soft flesh of her upper arm. She said she was very sorry afterwards, but she secretly kept the twin chips of diamonds that the Girl had winced out in pain on being pinched.

This relative comfort did not last long. The rich man came to her one day with sad eyes to tell her he had sold her to men in a richer country. The fee for which she was bought was a large sum, enough so that the rich man, who already had enough money for him and his children and his children's children to live like kings and queens without ever lifting a finger, doubled the amount he owned from the sale of the Girl's body.

They smuggled her in darkness for days and when she opened her eyes she thought she had died. Everything in the new place was clean and bright and white, even the people, who strolled in every morning in white coats and left every night in the same. They kept her in a white room in white pyjamas and did not allow her the luxury of shoes, but did allow her the use of a TV, which the Girl left on night and day for company. They gave her clean plastic buckets to piss and shit in and during the day they attached wires and things to her body and showed her sad movies to make her cry. They took her blood with small needles which, to their surprise, filled up with delicate dark droplets of rubies.

In the comfort of the lab the girl soon grew to be unhappy in a different way. All the days began to run together and she could not muster the strength to get up out of bed, or even to fight the strange people when they came wanting her for their experiments. When she refused to eat, they stuck needles in her arm, around which flower-shaped bruises blossomed, and in this way they kept her fed. One of the women in the white coats tried to warn her in their sharp language that they had ways of making her cry, but the girl closed her eyes and did not listen.

Shortly thereafter they brought her to a room with a large screen where they began to play a movie. The movie showed a dirty room with cracked walls and there were men speaking her language. There was a shape in the corner and a light was shone on the shape and the Girl could see it was a man, a man with a hood over his head. A hand reached out and pulled off the hood. And there was her brother! Filthy, bruised, his face swollen from beatings. And there was one of the men pulling back her brother's head so that his throat was exposed. And there was the man taking a knife and cutting deep into the throat with one pure clean motion, a movement that seemed too easy for one who was responsible for taking a life. Blood sprayed in a wide arc onto the camera lens. A lot of blood, but not enough to obscure the image of her brother flailing in his chair for the minutes it took for him to expire.

If the people in the white coats wanted the Girl's tears they now had them, but these were wet and tasted of the sea. They collected them faithfully hoping they would harden into the diamonds she had given before. They did not. For the first time in her life she pissed and shat normal refuse. Her monthlies did not give forth a tumble of rubies, but a thick stream of blood, and when they took more blood from her body, with needles and scalpels and knives even as they grew more and more angry with her withholding body, they succeeded only in staining their white, white coats.

They poked and prodded the girl until she thought she would die and when she was near enough to that state she was pushed out of a van onto a street in that strange country where she knew no one and nothing.

She tried to speak to the people she saw but they turned their eyes from her as quickly as they could. For hours she stood on the street, afraid and trembling and not one person in that place offered a kind word or a helping hand.

When the men in uniforms came for her she went with them, even though the word on their uniforms was close enough to the word in her language that she understood who they were and she knew they were not good men.

For days, in the jail, they used her body in a different way. There was no one coming for her, there never was for girls like her, and so when they tired of her they put her back on the streets to make her way in the world as best she could.

The last glimpse that anyone saw of her was in a border town, on the wrong side from the country where she had been born. It was a bad place for any person, a dangerous place for a woman especially. The story passed down from one man to the next was that she was seen whimpering in a corner, her body covered with scars, the wet drops of her tears staining the floor.

WOMAN INTO CLOUD

"Much like the way in which an opalescent pearl forms around
a grain of sand, the cloud could not exist without a seed of
imperfection. Under the right conditions when the purity of
water vapour meets sea salt, ash, or pollen it can mix to create
these kings of the sky. Knowing the humble origin of such
beauty it does not seem too much to imagine that any one of us,
when we return to dust, might yet dance among the clouds."

—*A Dictionary of Clouds*

I.

IT TOOK TESSA UNTIL the middle of her 43rd year to accept that she
had come to such an age. When she cleaned the condensation away
from the mirror to peer at her own reflection after a shower she did

not despise what she saw, but no longer could she pretend away the lines that broke across her forehead and the furrows etched between her eyebrows. Her hair was still lustrously, girlishly thick, but there were whites that sprouted from her temples, curling and waving away from their thick black sister strands, indicating in texture as well as colour that they were a different breed from the rest. Her body too was different from the way she remembered it being, a widened spread of the hips that had come from childbirth which she was still unused to and striae turning silver with age, remnants from her girl-hood and her girls.

There was nothing monstrous about her, yet the cruelty of aging was that sometimes Tessa felt monstrous in her own body. At night, between sleep and wakefulness, she could almost remember what it had been like to be a light-limbed flat-chested girl, to run so quickly in the summer that her feet slapping on pavement made her teeth rattle. She remembered what it had been like as a young woman, to look at herself when she saw her reflection in a shop window and to find her image pleasing. Now the softening skin around her jawline reminded her too much of what her parents had looked like as they slouched from their golden years into their twilight ones before slipping some-where else entirely.

Though Tessa wasn't really old she was at the age where she could see the old lurking in her body, a sinister undercurrent embedded in the skin. It was a point of no return, a point where she was no longer aging but simply getting older. It was too much for one woman to bear and yet, every day, Tessa endured it.

In addition to two children whom she called her own, Tessa had a husband of 15 years, a man with the improbable name of Brick Garnett. There was always hesitation in Tessa's voice when she called to her husband. A little niggle of doubt in her voice because she was always a little embarrassed of her husband's name. She thought it reflected poorly on her husband to have such a name and worse on his parents for choosing it. And then there was the bit of shame in herself for choosing to marry and have children with someone named after a pedestrian object. She had tried, vainly, very early in their courtship and again when they were married (and one final time after her first daughter, Tasha, was born) to address him by his surname. But by then she had already surrendered her own surname and taken his, becoming herself a Garnett. The little baby that she had carried in her body for nine months and insisted, once out, on being carried on Tessa's breast all through her first long sticky summer, the little baby that cried when her father held her, that baby was also a Garnett. So it made no sense at all to call him by a name they all held. By the time their second daughter, Rafaela, was born she was too tired for shame. Brick was Brick as he always was and always would be.

(There was of course the humiliating phase when Tasha learned that her parents had names and called out for her father with a piercing cruelty:

—Brick! Brick! Brick!

It was trouble enough at home, but one day Tasha said it in the schoolyard and that was it. For years afterwards Tessa had to face the faux friendliness of Tasha's friends' parents, all MPs and lawyers and doctors who thought it was *so* fascinating that her husband was a bricklayer, who always had an odd job to throw the way of the Garnetts. There was no good way to apprise them of the truth. The nervousness of Tessa's tongue and the pitying looks the other parents gave her made Tessa half feel she was lying when she spoke the truth. She took their cards, she wrote down their numbers, she promised her husband would come round, and she did her best, for years, to keep Brick away from other parents at their children's school.)

Brick was six years older than Tessa. It was enough of a difference that sometimes he mentioned songs he had listened to in his childhood or TV shows he had watched and she had no idea what he was talking about. It was so little of a gap that it came up in almost no other way. In the first few years of their marriage Tessa had been able to forget about the gap, but as they grew older she thought about it more and more. She liked it in some ways. Liked that Brick hit milestones before she did. He was middle-aged before she was. He had grey hairs before she did. She watched the baby fat fall from his cheeks, and while she staved off wrinkles with a sun hat and sunscreen, applied with diligence in the summer and winter both, she watched as the lines from too many summers and too many smiles radiated from his eyes and wrinkled his mouth.

At times she asked him if he was scared of the future, of dying or worse, being old and ugly, but these were not questions that troubled dear old Brick. True to his name he was steady, unsentimental, and rather oblivious.

In the worst years of their marriage right after Rafaela was born they had a fight. She was touched out from the baby feeding off her body and Tasha demanding to be cuddled. Brick, coming to her at night, the only time she had to herself, demanded that he too be allowed to touch her and in turn be touched. It was too much for Tessa and the night ended with her crying in her own arms, curled up beside their overflowing hamper, whimpering in a voice that didn't even sound like her own that she didn't know who she was anymore.

—You're a wife and a mother, Brick had said, his hand hovering just over her shoulder, the only time since the beginning of their courtship that he hesitated before he touched her.

Well. That was the point, wasn't it?

It was also perhaps why, a few years later, just as she was about to reach that milestone of her 40th birthday, Tessa had seriously considered having an affair.

Tessa would not have considered herself a flirtatious person yet there were flirtations she allowed herself, pleasant little smiles and lingering touches with men who didn't really matter. The summer before she turned 40 was different. There was a man who drew her attention in a dangerous way and, like the piece of chocolate she told herself she wouldn't eat every morning and had already consumed by noon, being near him was something she refused to resist. The affair candidate was the husband of a friend she did not particularly like, the mother of one of Tasha's friends who had orbited into her life years ago and unpleasantly refused to orbit back out, even when their girls no longer spent time together. As a husband he was less firmly embedded in her social circle but he was still there, lurking at the edges of children's parties, someone Tessa would have to interact with during and after the affair, if the flirtation progressed that far.

Tessa tortured herself about it for months.

The reasons in favour of going forward:

the man was tolerable

her "friend" had once implied Tessa was fat

the marriage between the friend and her husband was poor in a messy, obvious way that spilled out at family picnics and school events and made everyone else uncomfortable

the man flirted with Tessa every time he saw her

she wasn't going to be young forever

This last point was the one Tessa kept dwelling on, the one that was both the reason she craved the man's attention so baldly, why she thought of him thinking of her constantly and why she made up excuses to spend more time with the friend she hated, inviting herself over to the friend's house in an act of social impropriety that she normally would have blushed at. It was also the reason why she was too ashamed to respond when his hands lingered on her wrists or her waist for a few seconds longer than was strictly necessary. Because

Tessa still loved Brick and Brick still loved her. She could imagine him finding out that she had taken a lover and she could also imagine the look he would give her, the rebuke and shame of it, on finding out that she had done so because she was afraid of no longer being young. It was such a pitiful, pathetic, shallow reason that sometimes it kept her from properly fantasizing. So when the moment presented itself and the friend's husband drove her home one night after she claimed to have drunk too much red wine at the friend's house to manage returning home herself, instead of pressing her lips to her friend's husband's, Tessa merely unbuckled her seat belt and hopped out of the car. She made the walk from the car to her front door on mercilessly steady legs and when she got inside she was greeted by two little girls wondering where she had been.

So instead of having the affair Tessa thought on it. She thought and thought and thought on it for so long that her birthday passed (a tragically uneventful day on which she cried in a bathroom stall at work and came home to a strawberry cake that the girls had picked out, knowing full well she hated it). Then it was winter and everyone had the flu and then Tessa's brother announced he was separating from his wife, and then he wasn't, and then it was spring and with it came the news that the friend Tessa didn't like very much was divorcing her flirty husband who had in fact cheated on her, with the babysitter of all people.

—What a sad, pathetic cliché, Brick said when he heard the news.

Tessa told him to shut up.

In fact for a week after hearing the news Tessa told everyone to shut up. She was short with her daughters, her husband, her brother and her sister-in-law, who announced once more they were separating, and all the people at work. She had all her life been one of those people who prided themselves on being even-tempered and that week she found herself telling a cashier that she couldn't believe that she was smart enough to remember to breathe, just because the poor thing had accidentally run one of Tessa's items through twice.

No one but Tessa knew it was because she was grieving the non-existence of a relationship with a man she barely knew. It should have been *her* cliché, *her* sad midlife crisis. She should and could have wrecked her sad, fake friendship with a woman she could barely stand and her functional marriage with a man she still loved in a steady and unassuming way and instead she had hesitated.

And then the weeks turned into months and the months to years and there was always something. Work to go to and children to cuddle and dinner to make and sex to occasionally have. Life happened and she didn't think of the man she hadn't had an affair with at all, not even when she saw the friend she didn't like at birthday parties minus her spouse, unpleasant as ever as her eyes travelled up and down Tessa's body, calculating each curve and bump and lump that Tessa had.

By the time she was 43 Tessa could perhaps have picked him out of a lineup but would not have remembered his name. True to what Brick had told her she was, at last, a wife and a mother. She told herself she was happy that from this point onward, nothing about her would ever change.

> ". . . as every novice first learns and every nephophiliac well knows almost all cloud activity occurs in the troposphere with one notable exception . . ."
>
> —*A Dictionary of Clouds*

Rafaela was Tessa's darling, her baby, her last. When Rafa asked Brick what she had been like as a baby he told her stories of a holy terror who fussed and screamed and wanted all the attention in the world. What

Tessa remembered of her babydom was how she had looked just like a doll as she slept, like a baby doll with smooth perfect skin, her cheeks taut with the fat of breast milk, and long dark lashes thick as a paintbrush that fluttered as she slept. More than anything what she liked was to be held and cuddled, and Tessa had found these requests easier to indulge than the way Brick would proposition her in the first year of Rafa's life, groping and pushing Tessa's body in ways that were thrilling when she desired him and repulsive when she didn't. But with the girls, and especially with Rafaela, it was different. Rafaela would curl at her side and cuddle down on Tessa's breasts and she felt a complete ease as her child's body relaxed into her own.

Sometimes she would look at Rafaela and think of how Rafa's little body was something that she had made which seemed both unbelievable and like the only thing she had ever done that was worth doing. Sometimes Rafaela would lift her head and tell Tessa that her heartbeat was too noisy and Tessa would feel a deep sorrow knowing that her heart wouldn't always be beating for her daughter to listen to.

So yes, even though she loved both her daughters, in her cor cordium it was Rafaela whom she felt closest to and Rafaela whom she worried over the most. So it was natural, expected even, that when Tessa came down one morning as a cloud, it was her dear Rafaela who noticed the change in her mother first.

Tessa floated down to breakfast, a thick fog, and enveloped the kitchen entire. The beautiful glass cabinet doors, a luxury from a different time which had come with the house, grew condensation as her cloudy sides brushed up against them. She pressed up against the ceiling, causing the plaster to bubble and buckle, and with her dewy wet self enveloped and partially cleaned the light fixture which Tessa and Brick had ignored for the last five years, always leaving the cleaning to another day. In her previous form Tessa had liked the kitchen. Now she found it oppressive. She was just wondering whether she could turn a knob and squeeze herself through the door to the back porch, or whether she was limber enough to slip drop by drop, through a crack in a window when her family came down the stairs, the girls first and Brick after, all still tied to their corporeal forms and expecting breakfast.

Brick gaped. Tasha screamed. Rafaela began to cry.

—Mommy, Rafaela said, for the dear good child recognized the cloud at once. Oh, Mommy, what have you done?

Brick and Tasha narrowed their eyes and took a second look.

Of course a cloud cannot talk, not having a larynx, a tongue, a mouth, or any of those physical elements necessary in the creation of sound. Still, they could tell that this foggy mass in front of them, this wet pulse that from the corner of their eyes looked white and from straight on changed hues, from grey lilac to peacock green, this was the woman whom they knew as wife and mother.

—Shit, Brick said and then covered his mouth with his left hand, the silver wedding band glittering around his ring finger. They tried so hard not to swear in front of the girls.

Of course the first thing Brick wanted was to get them into marriage counselling.

If she had still had eyes Tessa would have rolled them. If she had had a mouth she would have stuck her tongue out at him. As it was, she was a small newly formed collection of gravity-defying dewdrops and it took all her will to simply be, rather than try to figure out a way to react to Brick and his rather pedestrian reaction to her extraordinary metamorphosis.

Brick ushered the children upstairs and made several discreet phone calls before he located a counsellor who understood he had a problem of such severity that even being seen that very second was already too late. While Brick called and called in the living room, cursing at voice mail and stuttering his way through awkward circular conversations when he reached a real live human on the other end, Tessa felt herself begin to change even more. Both the kitchen, where Tessa, the little cloud, was located, and the living room, where Brick dialled again and again and again, were on the ground floor. They were connected by a dining room and the whole space flowed intimately from one room to the next with no doors to sever the space. So as Brick talked Tessa began to ooze herself forward. First she took up the kitchen entire, then she made her way into the living room. By the time Brick had completed his calls the couch he occupied was shrouded in a thick fog. Tessa occupied the entirety of the first floor of their home. It felt delicious.

For so much of her adult life, and in her girlhood even, Tessa had spent much time trying to ensure that there was less of her. She could first recall stepping on a scale at the urging of some of her friends at a slumber party. They must have been around nine years old. While she couldn't remember the exact weight or height she had been what she did remember was the feeling of relief that came from not being heaviest and the sharp, bitter disappointment in not being the lightest. In comparison to the other girls she had been directly in the middle of the pack, the number on the scale accurately reflecting that she was neither fat nor thin. That desire, not to be the fattest girl, not to be the one who took up the most space, had dominated so much of Tessa's life from that point onward. It was not so much the numbers on the scale or the numbers on her jeans that preoccupied her but their relationship in comparison to the girls around her, those she called her friends. In university she had once, shamefully, befriended a girl who was twice her size, a hulk of a girl who always sat with rounded shoulders to try to shrink herself. She had been shy but friendly enough, and though she had a wicked, bawdy sense of humour that she brought out for Tessa only, her real value was that she could always be counted on to be larger than Tessa. For this reason it was a short, abortive relationship, and when the one class they had together ended so had their friendship. For a few weeks the girl had sent emails and texts offering to reignite the flames of friendship through coffee dates and movie outings, messages to which Tessa had never responded. So Sandra stopped trying and disappeared, going off and doing whatever people who were not Tessa's friends went on to do. Tessa herself went on in the same steady way, neither fat nor thin, and though she always promised herself that *this* was the summer when she would lose 20 pounds and be, once and for all, *truly* thin, she had only ever managed to succeed in shifting the numbers on the scale higher.

But now that she no longer had a corporeal form, Tessa felt comfortable expanding. She remembered the horror she'd felt as her hips, of their own volition, spread outwards in her mid-20s. She remembered the anxiety after her body swelled and then deflated through her two pregnancies, each time leaving her just a little wider than she had been before. She had felt a deep sense of failure each time her body had refused to return to what she thought of as her regular weight which was in truth a number on the scale which hadn't described her since her early 20s. Now though she was vapour, quite literally lighter than air. And she wanted to expand. After filling the first floor she began to creep up the stairs. She wanted to see if she could fill the entire house.

It was Brick who put a stop to this by gathering his coat and wallet and phone and keys, the necessities of his life, and opening the door, telling Tessa they would need to get a move on, to hurry if they were going to make their appointment.

Tessa had the faint thought that it would be nice to tell him to shove it, but once more the problem of not having a voice presented itself. Instead she continued her creep up the stairs. It was only when a breeze from the outdoors swept into the house, thrilling Tessa's molecules as the wind shifted through her that she thought of what an open door meant: the street, the city, the great outdoors. The sky, of course, where it was only proper a cloud should be.

—Tessa, are you coming?

It was easy to reverse herself, to roll herself off the steps and press the fog of herself towards the door, eager for the outside where she belonged, eager for freedom and all of its possibilities. She imagined herself shooting up, up, upwards to where the other clouds lived.

Brick almost lost her, right there and then, for Tessa was not thinking of her family at all, only cloudy thoughts of ascension. She could taste what it would be like to rise when Rafaela, hungry after having been abandoned in all the urgency and fuss of the day, came out of her room and perched on the top stair peering down at the parents who had forgotten all about her.

—I love you, Rafa shouted from the top of the stairs.

The little cloud, which had been halfway out the door and rising, dropped abruptly quite low to the ground.

> ". . . in point of fact no different from a cloud, fog is only distinguished as such due to its low-lying nature and belongs to the cloud genus stratus. It contains 100 percent humidity and is known for causing issues with human visibility, creating conditions suitable for the growth of mould, and wreaking havoc with hair . . ."
>
> —*A Dictionary of Clouds*

The marriage counsellor had offices on the second floor of an ugly and squat building in the downtown core flanked on one side by a pharmacy and on the other by apartment housing dedicated to low-income individuals. Some of those low-income individuals sat smoking in front of the building and watched as a car, filled with what they thought was smoke, rolled up in front of them and tried to park. They watched as Brick rolled down the car window and the smoke poured itself out of the car and then began, rather sinisterly, to roll itself towards them. It moved in such a determined and inhuman way that the smokers began to tremble and take fright. Several of the smokers ran back into the safety of their apartments unwilling to chance an encounter, but the more foolhardy and nicotine addicted remained behind and were relieved to discover the smoke wasn't smoke at all. It was only a bit of fog, fresh and dewy on the face but heavy enough to dampen their cigarettes and make smoking rather difficult.

The smokers enjoyed it while they could but it wasn't long before the fog was ascending, floating gently in the air like a proper little cloud until a window on the second floor was opened and the cloud rolled itself inside the building.

Brick had wanted Tessa to float into the building and take the elevator up like a human should, but Tessa refused. Being inside the cramped car, pinned in by windows, had been a nightmare. So while Brick tried to bustle her into the building she merely let him wet his hands in her vapour until he tired himself out, admitted defeat, and went into the building his way. Then Tessa was able to enter the building her way, floating up to the second storey and waiting patiently until Dr. Marianne herself opened the window of her office and let Tessa inside.

Dr. Marianne was the type of woman that Tessa had always wanted to grow into. She was all angles, with sharp cheekbones and sharp knees that protruded from under her tights. She had steel-grey hair that she did not bother to colour and she listened with tented fingers as Brick explained, in increasingly hysterical tones, what the problem was.

The woman and the cloud waited until Brick had spent himself, which took quite a long time indeed. Then Dr. Marianne turned to

Tessa and asked her to explain what had happened from her own perspective.

The cloud hung in its corner of the room shimmering and white and dense and though it never ceased to move it never said a word.

—Do you see? Brick said triumphantly, jabbing a finger in Tessa's direction.

—Yes, I do see. You have a communication problem.

—I have a my-wife-isn't-a-woman-anymore problem.

Dr. Marianne leaned back in her chair, reflecting, her eyes narrowed into slits.

—I'm not sure that *is* the problem, Dr. Marianne said.

Tessa felt that she liked this Dr. Marianne. Liked her very much indeed.

Though Brick and his talk had occupied half of the session, the rest of the time was spent between Tessa and Dr. Marianne. Dr. Marianne had an unusually beautiful voice, deep and melodious, and she talked very slowly as she worked with Tessa to find a way for them to communicate.

Tessa could not speak, that much was clear, but Dr. Marianne was disappointed to find that neither could she write words in the condensation she left on the long windows that lined the office. Tessa could not organize her cloudy form into easily discernable letters or even shapes. What Tessa could do was expand and contract. She would move from left to right and up and down. At Dr. Marianne's instruction she filled up the entire room, causing Dr. Marianne's straightened grey hair to wave and curl, obscuring the vision of Dr. Marianne and Brick so they became mere outlines to one another.

Later she curled in on herself, tightening her vapour into thick fluffy loops that looked dense as cotton and was roughly the same size as a desk.

For their final exchange Dr. Marianne stood underneath Tessa with her hands outstretched and asked Tessa if it was possible for her to rain.

The room was silent as they waited and then came the soft rapping of rain droplets hitting the carpet.

—Extraordinary, Dr. Marianne said.

She closed her fists around the drops Tessa had left on her palms as if she could hold onto them forever.

In the end Dr. Marianne worked out a simple yes/no system. Tessa would contract for yes and expand for no. Brick was told he should be patient.

—This could all go away as quickly as it appeared.

Though Brick didn't like it, he agreed that they should leave the counselling session much as they had come in. So Brick left the offices first, heading towards the elevator, while Tessa waited for Dr. Marianne to open the window and allow her to descend. Dr. Marianne headed towards the window and hesitated before she opened it, lifting one finger to the condensation that still coated the window and dragging her finger downwards through it forming a crooked finger-thick line.

Tessa, who longed to be outside, was suddenly aware of how precariously vulnerable she was when she was indoors.

—May I ask you one thing before you go? Dr. Marianne said and the cloud in her office shrank into itself. What does it feel like not to have a body?

It was not a yes or no question and therefore Tessa could have been forgiven for not answering it properly. But she felt a change come over her at the question, a bolt of pure joy, and whatever she felt must have translated itself into her dewdrops quite well for Dr. Marianne looked at her and let out a little sigh.

—That's just how I thought it would be, Dr. Marianne said and threw open the window to let Tessa pour herself out.

Though Tessa had found Dr. Marianne quite enjoyable both as a person and as a counsellor she was not altogether disappointed when Brick told her they were never ever going back. Though they continued to use the yes/no contract/expand method introduced to them by Dr. Marianne, Brick declared the entire session utterly useless and Dr. Marianne a crackpot (and also, possibly, not enough of a crackpot).

—We do not have a marriage problem, Brick said. (Tessa didn't quite know if she agreed.) We have a physics problem. We need a physics professor. (Tessa most definitely did not agree.)

Before Brick called physics professors he did something he should have done much earlier and called his mother.

Unlike her son and grandchildren, Anne Garnett did not immediately see Tessa for who she was. When her son called her, frantic and speaking nonsense about clouds, she had come over expecting that either her son was having some sort of midlife-crisis-induced mental breakdown or that her daughter-in-law had finally left him. To find her daughter-in-law gone and a cloud levitating in the living room did nothing to clear up the matter.

—Are you sure that's her? she kept asking Rafaela and Tasha as the cloud hovered in a corner.

—It's Mommy alright, Rafaela said.

The cloud contracted a little.

—Getting smaller means I'm right, Rafaela said. I've finished my dinner; may I have ice cream now?

Anne would have said no, but the cloud contracted again and already Rafaela was getting up from her place at the kitchen table to place her dishes in the sink and opening up the freezer to have at the chocolatey goodness inside. It had been a long day for everyone. Anne decided to let it slide.

The physicists seemed more skeptical than the marriage counsellor had been. Three hung up on Brick right away, one in Montreal seemed friendly enough but then referred Brick to his colleague in a psychiatric facility. It took several days of trial and error with different universities and their faculties and a bit of careful word craft, but Brick eventually found someone in Toronto interested in his singular meteorological weather event who was willing to see him. The problem then was travel. It seemed to Tessa they had only to wait for a southwesterly wind to lift her up and blow her the right way. (Brick could travel by plane, train, or car as he so preferred.) But as if by osmosis the thoughts that Tessa had of rising up into the air, of dancing with her fellow clouds, of flying, seemed to fly into Brick's thoughts too. And they did not fill Brick with the same feelings of rapture which they aroused in Tessa. In fact, since their trip to see Dr. Marianne, Brick had not been willing to let Tessa out of the house at all. At night, while the rest of the household slept, including Anne, who had never left since being called in to offer her emergency maternal services, Tessa would have loved to wander out and explore. The children however could barely be coaxed to their beds, they would have clung to her had there been anything to cling to. As it was they cried salty, bitter tears and recounted dreams in which she evaporated under a particularly hot sun.

Brick was somehow worse. While the children could at least, when persuasion failed, be dragged off to their bedrooms, Brick spent his nights camped out on the first floor which Tessa now occupied almost fully. He would sit on the couch in the living room and he would watch her, watch the undulating mass of her, for hours. In the early hours of the morning though he fought it as best he could, his eyelids would eventually flicker and he would fall into a distracted and reluctant sleep. Then it was Tessa's turn to watch him, to see how he kicked in his sleep, fighting the rest he so badly needed. In the morning he would wake up with a jerk, a look of fear on his face, and only when he spotted her would his facial muscles relax as he realized that his cloud-wife had not managed to evade him yet.

Tessa began to hate him.

He began to check windows and doors obsessively when he thought she wasn't looking. Brick, who knew next to nothing about home repair, bought a caulk gun and began to seal every possible crack in the house, from the gaps around the windows and back door to imagined cracks in the ceiling.

—Winterproofing, he said out loud to the cloud that never said anything back.

One time on her way out the door to school, Rafaela turned on her heel and ran back up the stairs, looking for something she had almost forgotten. In her haste she left the door half-open. There it was: freedom. It was a fine autumnal day with the weather crisp and the leaves of the maple trees just beginning to turn their vibrant final hues before they fluttered to the ground. The sky was a perfect blue and through the open door Tessa could see white clouds up high and she felt a pull in her to join them.

And then the door slammed closed, her glimpse of freedom gone. Standing jealously in front of the door as if he had caught Tessa with the lover she had never taken was Brick, turning practically purple with rage. Tessa watched with distant interest. She was a gravity-defying medical miracle. She was the answer to some ancient riddle, something perceivable but untouchable. He couldn't do anything to her.

Then Rafaela came back down the stairs and because the poor girl still had the misfortune of a body she was the one who suffered instead of her mother. Before her feet could reach the bottom step Brick snatched her by the shoulders and lifted her in the air. She was such a little girl still that he could keep her there, suspended off the ground, as he shook her.

—You stupid girl, he kept saying as he rattled her. Don't you ever think of your mother?

Tessa rushed to them and enveloped husband and child in a dense misty fog. If she still had her body, her old one as it was, Tessa would have raked her nails against her husband's face to teach him better than to touch her child in that way. As it was, the soft wet mist of the cloud on his face, obscuring his vision, had much the same effect as pain would have had.

Brick let go of Rafaela and she stumbled as she landed, hitting the floor with a little thump.

Tessa in her anger fled. She fled up high, pouring herself up the stairs to the second floor, then reaching for more, up through the cracks around the door that led to the garret, rising above the boxes of Christmas decorations and old and abandoned sports equipment, pressing herself up against the sloping rafters, feeling the whistle of the wind calling to her in all the cracks and gaps Brick hadn't yet found with his caulk gun, wishing she could rise higher still.

In moments of total despair, when she had had a body, Tessa had wanted nothing more than to be as low as possible. As a girl she had spent many hours locked in the bathroom, her cheek pressed to the gritty floor, crying until she had nothing left to give and the tears and cries came out of her in tiny silent hiccups. She had spent many hours on the floor wishing only that she could sink lower still. Sink through the floorboards down into the dark half-finished basement, down through the dirt and the worms until she hit bedrock and could go no lower. That was what she had wanted in those days more than anything.

What she remembered of this time was the overwhelming sense of powerlessness over her own body. It was a place of potential hurt that she could never escape. It was always used against her.

Tessa had married Brick, in part, because even though he wasn't the most handsome man, even though she never did quite get past the humiliation that she had married a man named Brick, she had never believed he was capable of hurting her. When she had had the children she had always believed that they were safe from harm as well. Now, at the worst possible time, when she could do little to protect the children, she was no longer so sure of Brick's intentions.

". . . it would perhaps be useful for the cloudy-minded to consult a cyanometer, a circular shaped instrument used to measure the colour of the sky and useful as an indicator of what sort of cloud conditions one might expect to form in the atmosphere . . ."

—*A Dictionary of Clouds*

On a certain morning, not long after Tessa had turned into a cloud, the news noted a strange pervasive fog which the Weather Network had not predicted. It was Tessa, who at first rolled low beside her family. There was a wild freedom to the open air, to stretching herself vast and thick as far as she was able. If before she had felt a thrill at being able to fill the first floor of her house she now took pride as she chased the family car, growing all the while. At first she was as wide as the house they lived in, then as wide as the avenue entire, then she was wider than the highway, wider than what would have counted as several city blocks. The feeling of letting herself unfurl to her full expanse was intoxicating.

The direction they were headed, up north, among the pines, was pure cottage country. Tessa had always held a small bite of envy towards those who owned their own cabins and shacks and therefore had no need to rent. Over the years she had looked at real estate from time to time, but Brick had vetoed even the most economical of cabins.

—It's not practical to own, he said each time she fell in love with a lakefront property. It was always the staging that got to her, canoes artfully hung over fireplaces and Bay-striped blankets thrown over well-worn couches. She knew he was right but she never stopped looking, even after their daughters were born and owning a property that they could only use for a quarter of the year was no longer something impractical but something they absolutely could not afford.

It was ironic then that it was now Brick who insisted that they go northward.

After she had seen Brick shake Rafa like a rag doll Tessa had spent what felt like hours up in the attic. She would have stayed there forever had she not heard his steps as he ascended the small crooked stairs that led to where she was. Each time his boots met a step they caused the old wooden boards to sing in protest.

When he finally got to the landing Brick let out a sigh that half hid that he was out of breath. Tessa thought it was another sign of the aging he pretended so valiantly not to notice.

—I wasn't sure you'd be here, he said.

It was hard to see anything in the dim attic, and Tessa didn't have eyes, but she was sure that Brick had been crying.

He turned and wiped the dust off a stack of cardboard boxes and succeeded only in stirring it up. A grey little cloud rose and merged with the dew of Tessa's body, and it caused her to grow and multiply.

With a sigh Brick sat on the boxes anyway, half collapsing them under his weight and then began fiddling with his wedding ring, a sign of nervousness she had never seen in her husband before.

—A guy at work has a place, Brick began.

Brick had had to spin a fiction to get use of the place, but when he intimated that he had marital troubles, the co-worker arranged for the family to stay there for free. It was the off-season of course and the insulation in the place was shoddy at best, but Brick believed that going there was the best thing they could do.

Tessa wanted to ask if Anne would be there and, as if he heard her, Brick looked up.

—Mom isn't coming. I asked her to go back home for now. I just want it to be you and me and the girls. It'll be good for us to have some time while we figure things out.

He looked up at her and Tessa could see the faintest hint of pink around his eyes.

—Do you agree?

Tessa curled up into herself, making herself as small and compact as she could even when it was clear that the answer was an unambiguous yes.

Brick nodded curtly. Tessa waited for him to say something else, to apologize at the very least and tell her that Rafaela was alright, but it seemed that Brick had no intention of communicating further with her.

—We'll leave tomorrow, he said as he left, creaking back down those small fiddly stairs. There was dust all over the seat of his pants.

Tessa expected the ride to the cottage to be an uncomfortable awkward thing, but it was one of the pleasantest journeys she had had in her life. Brick, for perhaps the first time in their marriage, was forced to be responsible both for himself and for the children. He did not perform the task as Tessa or his mother would have to be sure. Neither of the girls were wearing matching socks when they left the house, nor were either of them wearing an outfit that was aesthetically pleasing. They were however both clean and comfortable and well-fed and that was not nothing. There were also several false starts that morning as Brick had to keep running back to the house to make sure that he had remembered to lock the back door, to turn off the stove, to bring his credit card and phone and keys.

In the end Brick managed it all and they were en route, winding their way out of the wide residential avenues that made up their neighbourhood before joining the highway and speeding with wild abandon towards their destination.

Tessa had been afraid, due to their earlier fight, that Brick would somehow force her to travel in the car with them. If it had been possible for her to have nightmares she would have had one of being cramped in a small dark box, every crack an escape she longed to take, every sliver of light an opportunity she would have to ignore. To expand in the car would be disastrous and risk blinding Brick and therefore injuring her girls.

In the end the fear of being smothered was one she did not need to entertain. For Brick, chastened by their fight, merely opened the front door wide for her that morning and allowed her to pour herself out into the open air. She floated for a while on the lower currents, restraining herself from following the pull of the upper airs urging her higher.

—I wish we had one of those godawful pink cars, he said looking at their sensible navy-blue sedan with some regret. It would be easier for you to follow us then.

That was how Tessa learned that he intended for her to follow alongside them. She felt something like a pang and understood that this was as close as he could come to apologizing for what he had done to Rafaela. It was not enough to make her forget, but it stirred something in her that reminded her of what it felt like to love.

For a few hours she rode low just behind her family, watching as Tasha and Rafaela, buckled into the back seat, kept turning in the car and trying to find her. At first, she would rush forward and kiss the back of the car and the girls would press their hands against the back window and draw hearts and flowers and their own initials in the condensation.

As the hours wore on the effort of staying low became painful to Tessa. She found that if she did not concentrate she soon began to rise and to fly. It was something she knew Brick would not like, and something that made the girls nervous, but nevertheless she found herself very deliberately allowing her mind to wander. Then she was up in the sky, much lower than any other cloud, but far enough away so that the car looked like a toy car, a car she could have easily held in the palm of her hand had Tessa still had things like palms.

Tessa had lived in Ontario her whole life and had not travelled the province widely. Still, she was surprised by how the appearance of the land changed when she rose high above it. She always thought of the North as a thick impenetrable forest, but up high she was disappointed to see how much the treeline had been shorn by humans. From above she could see that along the highway there was a thin fringe of trees, just thick enough to deceive the human eye into thinking a wild forest lay beyond it. From her great height Tessa could see it was an illusion that hid squared-off tracts of land stripped bald. Here and there she could see small patches where the land had been let be and the wildwood hadn't been razed. They were like strange geometric mini forests. The untouched trees unbelievably dense and tangled together, the border clearly defined as whatever sister-trees had once grown close by had been cut down and uprooted according to the sharp boundaries decided by man's laws.

No matter how high she flew, Tessa always kept a sense of the car. She followed it as it slowed down and began to wind through a neighbourhood filled with similar cottages, each situated far from the road and surrounded by a thin fringe of skinny pines so that, like the shrubbery around the highway, the area appeared more forest-like and less domesticated than it truly was.

The houses were newish, shingled with vinyl siding in off-white and beige, above ground pools pimpling the properties. They were nothing like the romantic cabins that Tessa had once imagined she would own, old-fashioned fantasies built of wood with stone fireplaces. Even as the car continued on Tessa did not hold out hope that the co-worker's cabin would be different. In the end she was right; the house may have bordered the lake, but it was just as ugly as the other houses in the neighbourhood. Tessa felt a deep reluctance to lower herself to the cottage, but she watched as the girls leaped out of the car, as they ran exuberantly in circles around the place, running towards the lake and finding the charming little dock that jutted out onto the water. After a few minutes she could see them looking skyward searching for and finding her. They were just as much her children as if she were still made of flesh and bone, they knew her in an instant and called to her, begging her to come and join them.

Tessa had never been anything but a city girl. Early in their marriage Brick had tried to persuade her to join him in camping and canoeing and at various times, attempting to be a good girlfriend and later a good wife, she had indulged him, but it was never something she truly enjoyed. It always seemed as though mosquitos and other pests had a taste for her blood and her blood alone. It was therefore not uncommon for Brick to return to the city needing nothing more than a bath while Tessa would be covered in red bumps that itched and bled. There was also always, no matter how carefully she planned, the possibility that menstruation would begin, leaving her feeling miserable and unclean until she could return home and take a long high-pressure shower under water she could adjust to near scalding. And then there was the possibility of burning. Though Brick himself was very fair and burned easily he somehow seemed never to be in anguish from it. Whereas every time Tessa allowed herself to be persuaded into some activity outdoors she would find the trip ending with a rush to the pharmacy where she would tearfully scour the aisles for anything with even a trace of aloe. Brick would be the one who applied the cold gel to her body in soothing strokes murmuring his apologies as she whimpered. Yet somehow those apologies never extended to remembering the sunscreen the next time he persuaded her on one of these outdoor adventures.

Now though Tessa didn't have a body to be bitten, to bleed, to burn. When the girls called to her she lowered herself down towards them, drifting towards the lake and spreading herself over it thickly until the whole thing was covered in fog.

No sooner had she settled on the lake than Tasha and Rafaela came running towards her as if she had called to them by their names. They had a canoe that they had unearthed from the bowels of the cottage and oars and life jackets too. She knew that Tasha had taken after her father in that way, that between Brick and the outdoor programs her school offered, she had become quite the outdoorswoman. Tessa was quite touched to see the skilful way that Tasha leaped into the boat and how she held onto the dock with her hands, steadying the boat as Rafaela timidly climbed into it, reassuring her sister as the boat swayed uneasily that it was quite fine, that the boat would not tip over.

Once Rafaela had settled in herself she, following her sister's lead, took up an oar, and the two girls began to head for the centre of the lake where the fog was thickest.

Though they were set quite far apart from one another, there were enough cottages lining the lake that it could not truly be thought of as private. Given the lateness of the season it seemed unlikely that there would be many prying eyes watching the lake but even if there had been the fog would have prevented them from seeing much. Tessa took a special pleasure in knowing that her girls were protected from the outside in this way. It was like they were paddling in their own private world and for some time the girls worked without speech, with only their breath and the satisfying sound of oars in the water cutting through the silence.

When they reached what they estimated to be the centre of the lake, Tasha instructed Rafaela to stop paddling and they drifted peaceably for a while, the canoe spinning in circles so slowly the motion was barely felt.

Rafaela trailed her fingers in the water and peered overboard, hoping to see a fish and being rewarded only with a glimpse of the strange green plants that reached from the unseen bottom to just below the top, never quite breaking the surface.

Between the rocking of the boat reminding their bones of the way they were rocked in their cradles as babies and the fog of their mother, surrounding them on all sides and making the sun a distant hazy flare the girls felt yawns bubbling up through their bodies and they began to slip into a liminal state, not quite sleeping yet not quite awake. In this spirit they drifted.

And then they saw it, coming out of the haze. They had floated into a gaggle of geese, arranged in pairs, with ducks swimming lazily in between them. The geese stared at the intruder floating among them. The girls stared back. Now and again a duck paddled close to the edge of the canoe, hoping for food. They were so close that the girls could see that their feathers weren't as sleek and neat as they appeared from far away but quite straggly and greasy.

Tasha began to count silently, keeping track with a finger which waggled quietly in the air as she numbered them off. Between the birds which continued to paddle and the fog which hid the animals quite well it was nearly an impossible task. By the time they had floated through the menagerie of birds Tasha had still not managed to count up all the animals.

They drifted on, surrounded by fog once again and then Rafaela began to giggle. Tasha told her to hush, but Rafa could not, and when at last Rafa let out a huge loud snort of laughter Tasha began to laugh too. The geese, hearing the noise, began to clamour in their unbearably loud way, a high-pitched cacophony that was unpleasant to the ear and caused the girls to pick up their oars in tandem and paddle away from the geese and towards the dock they had originated from.

—There must have been a thousand birds, Rafaela said.

—I counted 28!

Tessa, who was the fog and knew everything within it, knew that there had been 44 geese and 34 ducks, the majority of whom had sat perched on the far banks of the lake, resting before their long journey south.

The day on the lake with the ducks would be a memory the girls cherished for a long time, one memory they could clearly access when asked if they could remember with distinction a time when they were happy. It was a happy day for Tessa, one of the last ones she was to have for a good long while. For when the girls returned ashore and headed back towards the cottage Tessa thought nothing of joining them too. Tasha opened the door and Tessa thought nothing of following her little beloveds. She had been put so at ease by her hours of freedom, speeding high in the sky and floating low on the lake, it did not occur to her that it would be awhile before she was in the fresh air again.

The cottage was a single-floor habitat, the bulk of the space one large, porous room where kitchen bled into living room. That room was lit by unforgiving halogen bulbs with a floor made of cracked and peeling linoleum tiles that made Tessa shudder as she remembered what it felt like to curl up her toes in the cold.

Brick and the girls did not seem to find the space objectionable the way Tessa did. To be sure the small space suited their small bodies. Even though Brick was tall enough that simply by reaching a hand upwards he could brush his knuckles against the ceiling, he was still only a human man. The space was enough to shelter and contain him. After the lake being inside the cabin felt to Tessa like suffocation.

Tessa hovered in the common area as the girls went to their room and unpacked and as Brick took to the kitchen and assembled the simple fare, grilled cheese and oven fries, which constituted a supper.

She stayed with them as they ate and watched with indifference. She had no nose to smell and no stomach to grumble. Food, which in her other life had been comfort and pleasure in addition to simple basic sustenance, no longer held any appeal for her.

She watched as Brick tried and failed to start a fire in the poky little fireplace and waited patiently as he got the girls ready for bed, reminding them to brush their teeth, listening as the girls told him again and again about the birds, promising that tomorrow there would be fire, a bonfire outside in the firepit if he still could not manage to work the indoor one.

Tessa even waited patiently as he went into the girls' room and tucked them in. She pressed herself against the back door, waiting to be let out, watching through the window the silver sliver of the moon in the sky and her sister-clouds hanging in the night. She longed to join them.

But when Brick came out of the girls' room he wore such a cold look on his face that she knew she had misjudged him. There was another bedroom in the cabin, one they might have taken for their own if Tessa and Brick still slept together as man and wife. But as if nothing had changed, as if they were still in their home, Brick settled on the couch to watch Tessa.

He looked at her with such hate that Tessa knew she had made a grievous mistake in ever venturing into the cottage. He watched her for hours, until early in the morning as the birds awoke and made their morning call, he tumbled into a fitful sleep that lasted only a few hours before the girls woke him up and it was time for a new day to begin.

Brick kept his promises to the girls. He figured out how to work the fireplace, though the little cabin became so choked between smoke and fog that he had to put out the fire nearly as soon as he had started it. He let the girls go for long walks where they picked up pretty maple leaves off the ground, as large as Brick's head and crimson to the tip. At the end of the week he built a bonfire and they threw their trash into it and watched their old tissues and discarded food wrappers blacken and crinkle and shrink and transform into a black smoke that rose into the air and turned into nothing. And all through this time Brick never offered to let Tessa out, not once, not ever.

She wondered if he knew that she could leave at any time.

The cabin was solid, but like all things cursed to live through time it was aging, peeling apart at the corners. There were cracks and crevices and holes she could slip through at any moment had she so desired. And she did so desire it. She desired it more than almost anything. The only reason she stayed was because there was a part of her that could not bear to leave her girls.

They knew of course that something was wrong. Tasha noticed it first, and Rafa, no matter how valiantly she tried to believe that this was an ordinary vacation, was a sensitive child. She could sense the misery in the air. Tessa watched the smiles slip slowly from their faces day after day until they stopped appearing at all.

—I don't think Mommy likes being inside, Rafaela ventured once, keeping her eyes firmly on the drawing she was making. On the page there were two little scratched-in girls, a larger figure representing a father, and above the trio a cloud haloed their heads.

—Of course she does, Brick answered. He too kept his eyes slotted downwards. He was so busy avoiding Rafaela's eyes he did not notice that her eyes were avoiding his. Mommy loves being with you.

Tessa thought she was the only one in her family brave enough to witness this charade, but then there was Tasha, perched in the corner, her red plaid shirt somehow blending in with the hideous florals of the rust-coloured couch. Though she had a book open in her lap she was not looking at it. Rather she was merely thumbing the pages absent-mindedly, staring at her sister, who was so young and timid that she could barely mount a defence in her mother's name, and her father, who had the gall to lie to his children but not the temerity to look them in the eye as he did so.

Tasha was 12 and just hovering on the final edges of what it meant to be a child. She was as tall as her mother had been before the trans-formation but all sharp angles. Pin-straight legs and slim hips and flat as a board on top.

Once, the previous summer, Tessa had found her crying because two of her friends were already wearing bras and Tessa had taken her into her arms and rocked her back and forth and told her that it really wasn't so bad to be a woman. That in the end the changing body and the menstruation were things she would get used to. She had stroked Tasha's hair as she had talked, and when that failed to comfort her, she had combed the long dark hair out with her fingers and braided it neatly, the way she had when Tasha was a toddler with just thin dark wisps that could be braided in seconds.

Without Tessa quite noticing how or why, Tasha began to slow her tears so that by the time Tessa had finished the plaits, neither of which she had an elastic for, and both of which came undone when Tasha turned over to look at her, Tasha had stopped crying.

Her whole face was pink and flushed and dewy from the tears. She was pretty in her misery and Tessa felt her heart swell and wished she could do something, anything to protect her from all that was to come.

—What are you even talking about? Tasha said, staring at her mother wide-eyed.

In the face of her even and awful stare Tessa felt her heart stam-mer. She had a feeling like she was back in school and she was about to be called upon to answer something that she should have known and yet could not for the life of her remember.

—I thought you were upset, Tessa offered falteringly and then stopped unsure of how to go on.

—I want to get a bra, Tasha said snottily as if Tessa was an idiot. I want to get my period and be like the other girls. I don't want to be one of those weird freaks that doesn't hit puberty until I'm 17.

She said 17 in much the same way that Tessa said 65, an age so far away as to be ridiculous. Implausible that she would ever get there.

That evening, Brick tucked the children in and resumed his watch over Tessa. He had, over their time in the cabin, begun to relax. While he still watched over Tessa he no longer waited as long as he could before falling asleep. Instead he slept when he felt like it and fell into an easy and deep sleep, awakening with reluctance every morning, knowing that his unhappy, aggrieved wife would still be right where he had left her. Tessa did not know if he truly believed she couldn't escape him, but he acted as though he believed she were bound. That night, as always, he took up his position on the couch, but he very quickly tired of looking at Tessa. He shut his eyes and was asleep in an instant.

It took some time, but the door to the girls' room creaked open and a little girl crept out, her dark hair a tangled mess spilling over her shoulders.

It was Tasha, in her bare feet, tiptoeing across the chilled linoleum floor so she wouldn't wake her father.

She looked at her mother and then gestured to the door and together, mother and child (or rather child and cloud) made their way to the door of the cabin.

No matter how careful she was Tasha was not magic, she could not help but make some sounds as she loosened the bolt and turned the knob of the door. She did all she could to keep the noise to a minimum and so she was able to open the door wide and release her mother into the wild without waking her father.

Tessa threw herself out the door as quickly as she could, the promise of long-denied freedom making her impatient and lustful. Almost at once she unfurled herself wide as a yawn and rose into the air. It was a beautiful night, with the moon casting an indecent amount of light upon the earth. The sky was cloudless, apart from Tessa herself, and up high, dancing in the moonbeams, she felt the great pleasure of being.

Tessa was unsure of how much time she spent flying high above, but after a while she came out of herself enough to think of Tasha. She was still there, sitting on the cabin's wood porch, her arms tucked over her knees, her face pointed skyward. Her little face was illuminated by the moon so that Tessa could see the expression of great sadness that she wore. It was that sad expression that caused Tessa to remember herself and think of the great risk Tasha had run in letting her mother be free. She still remembered how Brick had shaken Rafa, how that one incident had led to the family coming here and her imprisonment. Everything in her being was calling to Tessa to rise and be free, but with a great effort of will she managed to find little gustlets of air, to follow their paths towards the earth and pour herself downwards. She went slowly and took more time than was strictly necessary to descend, savouring each movement she made. She took in the view both above and below knowing that the memories of the night would have to do for many days or perhaps weeks until Tasha thought to let loose her mother once more.

At last she was grounded, or as close as could be. She waited for Tasha to rise and open the door so they could both sneak in and pretend they had never left. Tasha merely stayed where she was, watching her mother. The child had something of Brick in her. Not just of the body, but of the face too. Her nose was a more delicate version of his own broad snub, and her forehead was an unlined miniature of his own. But the way Tasha looked at her did not remind Tessa of the way her husband had stared at her all those nights. There was nothing possessive in her gaze, nothing calculating or cruel. Tasha was looking at her mother with deep filial love.

Tasha had never been like Rafaela. Very early on she had shirked physical affection from Tessa. As she grew older and more tame she could sometimes be convinced to bear a hug or, God forbid, a kiss. There was always a sense of submission in these exchanges. She would hold herself very stiff and if Tessa forgot which daughter she was dealing with, if her embrace lingered too long or she began to pepper kisses on Tasha's cheeks, Tasha was adept at reminding her just who she was. She would push her mother away very firmly.

Now on the porch, Tessa found herself wanting to give Tasha a hug. Wanting to take her daughter's thin body in her arms and crush her against her chest until Tasha wriggled away from her and uttered her famous That's enough. Since she had no arms and no chest and no body at all Tessa settled for the next best thing. She swirled all around her daughter so that Tasha was lost in a fog.

If her mother had had a body in that moment Tasha would have allowed herself to be held, but instead, recognizing the gesture, she closed her eyes and reached out her arms, trying to be at one with the fog as best she could.

It was Tessa who ended the moment. She began to curl herself up smaller and denser until slowly, like a veil being lifted, the clear night came back to Tasha and the moonlight poured down upon her.

Tasha lowered her arms and turned and saw the cloud of her mother, densely packed, hovering by the door and waiting to be let back in. And then Tasha did a curious thing. She shook her head.

—No.

Tessa did not understand at first. She shifted towards the door to indicate where they must go and was surprised when Tasha shook her head again.

—No, Momma, Tasha said once more. Don't worry about me and Rafa. We'll be fine. I'll explain it to her and she'll understand. You belong to the sky now.

If Tessa had had a mouth she would have argued with her daughter. She could perhaps have convinced Tasha and half convinced herself that she belonged in that cabin with the children she had borne and the husband who wanted to control her. She did not have a mouth though and so her will to argue died with her lack of ability to do so.

She looked at Tasha with her sorrowful eyes and her jaw set with determination and she saw the wisdom in what she was doing and the grace with which she had done it.

There was nothing for Tessa to do but accept the kindness that had been bestowed on her with equal grace. So she rose, higher and faster than she ever had before, unfurling in a great magnificent display.

The little girl looked up at the cloud up in the sky made of dusky lilacs and navy greys billowing and moving and changing shape from one minute to the other. For a little while the cloud stayed directly overhead, blocking out the light of the moon and turning the night a uniform grey. Then, very swiftly, as if blown by a fierce wind, the cloud sailed off, leaving the little girl shivering on a strange porch in a cold and cloudless autumn night. Though she knew the night would be clear and the day would be as well, Tasha Garnett stayed on the porch and looked up at the stars until the dawn began to break and then she tiptoed back into her bed on cold feet with toes as chilled as icicles.

II.

"... presenting difficulties with how to measure cloud size. Thus the okta was created. As its name suggests it uses an eight portion system for measuring cloud coverage in the sky. Though the okta system fails to cover the depth of a cloud it is useful in other measures, for example ..."

—*A Dictionary of Clouds*

For their honeymoon Brick had thought it might be romantic to wander Tessa's ancestral lands and go to Mexico. It was not an idea that had brought Tessa much joy at the time. She hated the idea of going to resorts, finding them too like an odious vestige of colonial times when the brown were forced to cater to the white. In the end Brick's notion of romanticism had won the day while her aversion to resorts had meant they spent an unromantic few weeks in D.F. visiting with her family and trying to avoid the crowded city centre. The only touristy activity that Tessa consented to, in the end, was a day trip to visit the pyramids. Brick was delighted to find they were scalable and Tessa agreed with him that it would be wonderful to climb to the top. But less than halfway up her body began to fail her. From the base of the pyramid the top had not looked so far; less than a quarter of the way up her thighs began to tremble out of fear. The steps were narrow and crooked and there were no railings to hold onto past the quarter mark. Brick kept barrelling ahead, looking back occasionally to see where his new bride was, growing exasperated at her lack of progress. In the end Tessa told him to go ahead without her as she struggled upwards alone.

The higher she rose, the more each step cost her. She felt as though she had to negotiate each hard-won step with her body, at times coaxingly telling it there was nothing to be afraid of, at other times berating it for being so weak and foolish, for quivering with so much force she had to pause for minutes at a time, soothing herself, before she could persuade her body to take another step.

She made it halfway up the pyramid before she was forced to stop. Her body would not listen to reason and it would go no further. It insisted on plastering itself firmly against the steps and watching, in horror, as other tourists, in sun hats and visors, with children even, bounded up and down the steps leaving her alone, stranded, in her own private pain.

Though consciously she knew that eventually Brick would come down and hopefully retrieve her, Tessa's body was quite willing to let her die there. She remained trembling against the stone of the pyramids, unable to descend or ascend until an elderly white couple found her. The woman noticed her first. She was climbing down the stairs in her own slow way. She would first put one foot down, wait until she was assured of its position and then have the other foot join her. For a few seconds she would remain there, solidly two-footed, before she began the whole process over again, reaching out one exploratory foot for the lower step and allowing her weight to wholly transfer there before bringing forth her second foot to join the rest of her. Tessa first noticed the woman when her feet were at Tessa's eye level. It took the woman some time before she reached the step where Tessa stood shaking.

Though she didn't remember doing it and didn't think it was really possible, Tessa knew she must have moved her head in some way. For when the woman occupied the same step as Tessa she did not continue on down the steps. Instead she moved towards Tessa. She had on an ugly white visor and khaki Bermuda shorts which emphasized rather than hid the lower pooch of her belly. When she got to Tessa she took out a bottle of water which was clipped to her belt and offered it to her. Tessa shook her head no (for though she was dying of thirst the thought of moving her body, of taking one of her hands away from the pyramid and reaching through air towards something was too much coordination for her body to even bear thinking of). The woman took a long, slow pull from the bottle herself.

—Mucho sol, the woman said, pointing at the fiery orb above them.

Her Spanish was bad. *Mucho* came out as *much-o* and *sol* sounded more like *sole*. Tessa was grateful for her heavy accent, she knew from the way the woman spoke that she was an anglophone.

—I don't know how to get down.

Even Tessa's voice was a series of trembles. It embarrassed Tessa. The woman merely nodded.

—Heights. Some people are afraid they'll jump and some people are afraid they'll fall. Now you, you look like a faller.

She turned to the man beside her, a white-haired man about her age, sporting matching Bermuda shorts and a khaki-coloured fishing hat instead of a visor. She handed the man her water bottle.

—We've got to help this young woman down, the woman said to her husband. She's got the fear in her.

The man nodded curtly and without further discussion took a step down and then turned and waited for his wife.

Tessa opened her mouth to argue that her body simply couldn't, but the woman had already caught hold of Tessa's hand in her own bony, dry one. She twined her arm through Tessa's and was taking one step down and Tessa moved with her, afraid that if she did not this woman, rather than being her salvation, would drag her down with her. By the time she had got both feet on the next step she barely had time to marvel at the fact that she had not fallen, that she was one step lower than the height she had been, because the woman was already gearing up to step down again, tugging Tessa's body forward with her, and again Tessa had no choice but to follow. One step and then another. They went on in that shuffling, childish way, as if they were three old people instead of two old people and a young woman. The man led the way. He could, Tessa noticed, take the steps in the normal way, putting his left foot on one step as his right went down to meet the next. He was patient though, he never went more than two or three steps before he stilled, turned around to check on the slow progress of Tessa and his wife. Occasionally he looked out at the view and sighed, but it was a sigh of contentment and not of annoyance.

When they got to the first quarter platform the fear rushed away from Tessa's body so abruptly it was as if it had never been there at all. There were no trembles or shakes left in her, when she reached for the next step she found herself not bothering to look down to make sure it was there. Instead Tessa looked backwards, up towards the summit of the pyramid, and wondered what on Earth was wrong with her. It was a beautiful day, the temperature moderate, the sun bright and bold with only a few puffy white clouds up in the blue sky above. The pyramid was so small that in theory it wouldn't take more than two or three minutes at most for Tessa to conquer. But it would have in actuality taken Tessa hours to walk those steps, if she was capable of it at all, and she knew it. Rather than attempting to rise again, she continued her descent. By this time she was well enough that she could take the stairs normally. Now she led the way, offering her hand to her rescuer, helping her along, one step at a time until together their feet met the sandy soil of the earth where the collective beat of tourists' feet had long since stamped grass out of existence.

At the base of the pyramid she bought some overpriced bottled water and talked with the couple for a moment.

They were retired and the pyramids of Teotihuacan was one of a series of locales on a list they had made long ago when they were newlyweds and were just now seriously beginning to visit. They were pleased to hear that Tessa was on her honeymoon and the gentleman of the couple even offered to go back up the pyramid once more to see if he could locate Brick and bring him back to her. Tessa assured him it was not necessary. And it wasn't. Eventually Brick came trundling up beside her. She had been made so tranquil by the older couple and she was so used to Brick always being there, by her side, that she did not register his shadow falling across her or the warmth of his body by her side. It was only when the couple flicked their eyes away from Tessa that she turned her head to see what they were looking at and saw beloved Brick looking confused.

—I couldn't find you.

He then collapsed on the bench beside Tessa and took one of her hands delicately in his own and brought it to his mouth and kissed it.

Tessa felt a frisson going over her whole body. The day had been too much. She was not used to the heat or the altitude, she had been vanquished by height, and now this romantic overture from Brick was so out of character that it was confusing. For just a moment blackness crawled over Tessa's vision and when she woke up she was in Brick's arms on the ground, and the older woman who had rescued her was sprinkling water on her face, pouring it into her palm and then using her fingers to flick it onto to Tessa.

Sunstroke, Brick and the other couple agreed. After that everything moved quickly. There were hasty goodbyes and Brick helping Tessa to walk back to the car, one arm firmly around her waist to support her.

Later that afternoon after she had been properly rested and watered, Tessa tried to explain the fear that had caught her up in its web and held her prisoner at the side of the pyramid. That moment between total fear and the release of it was something that fascinated her and she kept trying to explain it, using words to describe something that could really only properly be felt. Brick, while sympathetic, was more interested in his wife's body. And Tessa was more than willing to let herself be distracted. The body, it turned out, was not built to hold onto fear or pain. The feeling washed away and became only the memory of a memory.

Her fear of heights she watered down, a fact about herself that she laughed at.

A few months before Tessa had morphed from human to cloud a friend who worked at an elementary school had offered to sneak her onto the roof of the century-old school to see the magnificent view of the surrounding parks, especially beautiful in the thick fullness of spring.

—Oh, Tessa's afraid of heights, Brick had said before she could open her mouth to speak, closing the matter for her.

The opportunity slipped away; they soon talked of other things.

". . . by this author's estimate there are easily over 100 different names for individual winds and each one holds the capacity to usher forth a drastic change in atmosphere or usher forth a storm of clouds . . ."

—*A Dictionary of Clouds*

Now that there was no body to hold her back, the height of the sky felt magnificent and free. Though Tessa had never flown that high before, not unless being on an airplane where she was too terrified to look out the window counted, she felt at ease in her soul. There was a sense of déjà vu attached to the feeling though, as if freedom was something she had once had, long ago, and been forced to forget out of necessity. In the sky what she loved best was to let the wind take her where it willed.

Winter came quickly that year. No sooner had the leaves changed to their brilliant colours with not a fleck of green in sight than the snow began to drop. The result was a treeline of fiery red with branches a brilliant and blinding white. Up in the sky Tessa contributed to the snowfall enjoying the way her vapour turned into thick flecks which tumbled away from her and fell all over the city.

For a while she remained there, close to her former home and her former daughters, who had been ushered from the cottage back to the city shortly after Tasha had released her. She hid from the girls, knowing that if they called to her she wouldn't be able to resist them. Though there was nothing he could do to her, she hid from Brick too. In the daytime she floated about different parts of the city, surprised that there was still so much to discover in a place she had lived her whole life. There were more trees than she thought possible in a place so preoccupied with buildings for bodies, scraggly brown tangles of them reaching heavenward as their leaves finally drooped and disappeared under the weight of snow while the pines remained ever green and took on thicker coats in the winter chill.

The long river that served as a border and delineated Tessa's city from the sister city across the way slowed to a trickle as snow turned to ice and the ice grew wider and wilder, small floes drifting slowly into others until they formed a broad sheet like a glassy continent that nearly covered the river from one bank to the other.

Though her days were for exploring, at night she found herself drifting homeward to the place that sheltered the only beings on Earth she still had it in her to care about.

From up high she watched the neighbourhood, peaceful in the night. It was a sleepy place, a place built for families, families with children, families whose bedtime habits were built around the needs of the aforementioned children and the drooping and exhausted caregivers greedy for sleep after long days. So though occasionally she saw a night owl going for a late night walk or smoking an illicit cigarette she saw almost no one else and absolutely nothing of the girls, who lived their lives in the daytime only. The only thing of note she saw in all the time she watched over the house was that the roof was missing more shingles than she had realized and would need to be repaired soon, at some expense.

But what cares a cloud for shelter or shingles or even money. From high above she saw not only her house but the winding little streets she had walked on for years to get to and from the handful of places that were habitual to her. The bus she had taken to work every day still ran its same course hour after hour. The parks she had played in with the girls were still there, transforming into white squares as winter snow eroded the playable space. Further on were the places she had played in as a child, the small park which was cut through by a canal. The long winding canal which the city was so famous for (the longest man-made canal in the world, signs boasted) was now drained of water and looked like a scar cut into the earth. Soon it would be flooded again, carefully, so the water could turn to ice and the ice turn the world's longest man-made canal into the world's largest outdoor skating rink.

The cloud drifted along these paths and others, remembering when she was just a little girl and she and her friends had climbed into the drained canal and walked in muck, looking for hidden treasure that might have been left behind. When they tired of poking at rusty shopping carts and plastic shopping bags grown papery and wispy in the elements, they had tried their best to climb back out and found, to their horror, that they couldn't. It was only when the group of girls laced their fingers together and launched Tessa, the tallest, upwards that she had finally been able to grasp the edge of the wall with the tips of her fingers. Just barely she managed to lift herself up and back onto land. Then it was her turn to return the favour. Her arms still burning with the effort of pulling herself upwards she had rolled over onto her stomach and weaved her body under the bars of the railing that bordered the canal. She had reached down, her numbed and reddened fingers straining towards the next girl's muddy fingers, already reaching up to meet her own. It took several tries before their hands successfully met and then Tessa was pulling with a strength she did not know she had, using muscles she had never used before, her back legs kicking for purchase as she tried to lift the girl up rather than be dragged back down. She had not believed it was possible as she was grasping the girl's hand in her own, the mud turning into an unctuous sludge between their mingled fingers, that she could help lift her friend up to the edge. But it was possible, she was able to raise the girl enough so that she was able to grab the lowest rung of the railing and, with great effort, heave herself up the way that Tessa had before her.

They rolled away from the canal edge and laid on their backs for a moment, every muscle sore, shuddering out little laughs of relief, shocked that they had done something so stupid as to willingly jump down into the canal and shocked that, once stuck, they had had the strength to get out of it. Then they reached down and did it all over again, till all the girls were lifted up again.

It had been a happy memory before but Tessa grew tired of remembering the life she had lived down below. She allowed herself to drift farther and farther, to rise higher and higher and one day, when it had been weeks since she recognized the land down below, she felt the chilled fingers of a cold wind urging her along and, finding no reason to fight against its gentle persuasion, allowed herself for the first time to soar and mingle with the other clouds above.

". . . a rare type of non-tropospheric cloud, noctilucent clouds exist in the mesosphere. As their Latin name suggests they are characterized by their eerie shimmer and visible only after night during the brief period when our sun begins

to chase away the dark, known as astronomical twilight.
There is no scientific recording of their existence before
1885 though . . ."

—A Dictionary of Clouds

Like so many children born to a society that thought of itself as modern,
Tessa had been raised without a god. Yet the first time she flew she felt
that this was as close as she had ever come to experiencing heaven.
She mingled with the other clouds and saw that while the below was
peopled with the familiar, up above there was nothing between her and
the vast blue of space. The sun poured its light over her and the rest
of the clouds and painted the ever-changing, ever-shifting expanse in
colours from rose to gold. It was enough to humble her to the beauty
of all the trite religious imagery of winged angels strumming at lyres
while balancing atop white pillows. This was as close to a celestial
kingdom as the Earth could produce and she felt herself swell with joy
and pride knowing that she was, without a doubt, a part of the beauty.

Tessa allowed herself to mix and become part of the stratiform and
felt serenity at being part of something so wondrous. Yet even in her
happiness there was a pinprick of unease. There were times, too few
and too far between, in Tessa's before when she had felt something akin
to joy. When a smile cracked her face involuntarily so that she hadn't
had time to worry about the way her upper lip disappeared when she
smiled. Or, rarest of all, those moments when she was so happy that
she laughed, ridiculous loud peals of joy that set off everyone around
her. Both times after she had had the children when she was assured
that they were both safe and breathing she laughed. She laughed even
as she lay on the birthing bed exposed and bloody and raw in front of
Brick and a doctor and nurses who had seen the most intimate parts
of her yet would soon be strangers to her. She had laughed when the

children were brought to her even though her body was still shaking from the contractions and each laugh felt like it was shaking her open.

Tessa, watching the clouds, being a cloud, felt that her joy was tainted by her inability to express it by laughing. For the first time since she had become a cloud she regretted not having a body.

It was lonely too up there amidst the beauty. She could intermingle with the clouds, passing above them and beside them, mingling their dewdrops with her own, gathering the swirling dust the wind brought to her, and feeding on it to change her form, until she was no longer sure if she was the thing that she had started out as or something else entirely. She wondered if the children would recognize her now. She wondered too if the other clouds were only as they appeared: pretty and suspended drops of vapour and nothing more. Or if they were as she was: women turned into clouds. Women who had been unhappy and dissatisfied with their own bodies who had decided one day to become something else and then had simply done so.

She tried to talk to the clouds but she encountered the same problem she had had with humans. No tongue, no teeth, no speech, a painful lesson learned again. The attempts she made at communication, at shrinking herself down or puffing herself up or, in one act of desperation when she felt adrift and lonely, of raining, evoked no conclusive results at all. Sometimes, gathered on the wind, they fled from her. Sometimes she chased them and watched with horror as they dissipated in front of her.

For while the other clouds sometimes responded in kind it was impossible to tell whether they were reacting with real intention or if they were simply doing as clouds did.

If anyone had told her before that it was possible to tire of such beauty she would never have believed it. But tire she did.

After a time even the sight of the sun setting or rising, dyeing the landscape in bold colours, was not enough to soothe her. When the sight of the sun rising, turning the clouds around her a brilliant red, evoked in her only a deep feeling of boredom, she knew it was time to move on.

So she floated away to find her peace where she could.

Even at her immense size, even carried off by winds so strong they moved her across cities in minutes, even so, the world was immense and Tessa the cloud was only a small part of it. Left to her own devices she could float sulkily in the same spot for days. When she could, she caught a wind and allowed herself to be blown away. In this way she saw the world.

At night it was sometimes difficult to tell the difference between the stars, pebbled in the velvety sky and bright as diamonds, up above and the cities, which spread out in bursts like exploded suns, down below.

There were things she saw which recalled to her moments of her old life. Oftentimes from down below she would see a person turn their face skyward and look at her. Sometimes they would take a little rectangle out of their pocket and aim that at her. Phones, Tessa remembered. They were taking pictures. When she was younger she had willingly mugged for the camera at birthdays and parties. Her father was usually the one wielding the thing, her mother always somewhere in the back hiding. After her death it had been Tessa's job to find photographs to include in the memorial and somewhere in the haze of her grief she was disturbed that the vast majority of them showed her mother half in profile, her back humped protectively as she curled herself inwards, one shoulder raised up to her ear as if she could use her body to block out the camera. It saddened her to see her mother so uncomfortable but it also reminded her painfully of herself. Half the pictures Brick had taken of her were of her hand reaching out towards the lens, trying to block the camera as if she were a celebrity and he were a particularly aggressive paparazzo. Tessa wondered if the children had any pictures of her facing the camera or if all that had been preserved for them were these shots that displayed her discomfort with the camera, a truer portrait of her spirit than if they had captured her face.

How ironic then that now strangers could take pictures of her whether she wanted them to or not. At her most uncomfortable she had spent hours scrolling through pictures of younger, more beautiful women, women who made their money off their looks, and how she had envied them their confidence and their beauty. Now here she was, beautiful and photographed, and the passiveness with which she was forced to endure someone else's gaze, someone else's lens, infuriated her.

So she moved on.

She moved to the forests and found them butchered beyond recognition. There were pockets of green everywhere around the world to be sure, but far less than she would have expected, and all bore marks of the cruelty of humans, the earth hacked and scarred in a way that would have caused an ache in her heart had she still had one. She moved on to deserts, seeking their arid emptiness but she found them more populated than she could have imagined and the hopeful looks that the flora and fauna gave her, their faces upturned, praying for rain and salvation, made her feel guilty. She rained on them until she was less than half her size and then, like a coward, sped away on a warm wind.

In school she had learned that most of the Earth's surface was water which was a fact like any other, easily understood but not felt. When she tired of the lands, she took to the oceans. She understood that there were whole lives lived and fought under the surface but it was a joy not to see them and not to have to think of them. The sea roiled and it was beautiful and fierce and awesome in a way that would have frightened her if she had been a little body but which she was indifferent to as a large fearsome cloud that could never be touched, no matter how high the waves licked upwards.

Occasionally she saw big ships patiently hauling cargo, making their journey across the vast space from one shore to the next. When the storms came these ships were tossed like toys in a bathtub and she quickly moved on, not out of fear for the passengers but out of weariness at seeing anything that was human.

Yet there was no escaping it. The traces of humanity were everywhere.

Some time after she came to the ocean, Tessa found herself flying past an area into which fish and birds ventured but did not come back out. From high above the area looked like the rest of the ocean but Tessa knew there was something strange about this place, this dead zone. Though she knew there was nothing on earth that could harm her anymore she felt echoes of fear. She flew low, turning herself into a fog that was kissed by the ocean spray which rose up to meet her.

The dead zone wasn't made up of water like any other. Instead it was a sludge made of detritus which she recognized from that other life. She recognized the sheer Lucite of toothbrush handles rendered in all the synthetic colours of the world. There were menstrual pads, startling white as the blood that had clotted on them had been dissolved by the ocean and washed clean. Trash bags that had come into the world before Tessa was even a possibility to her parents were worn as thin as tissue paper. There were plastic bottles everywhere, flattened and torn to sharp ugly shards and bottles that sometimes managed to retain their entire shape. Just as Tessa was a swirl of droplets shifting and changing in the wind, so was this zone an unholy bastard brew of everything the world had created and unthinkingly cast aside.

Tessa was a cloud and nothing could hurt her, but still once she saw what she had seen she caught an updraft and rose back up into the sky. Without much thought she allowed herself to be carried far away until she reached the shores of a distant and unfamiliar land and decided to see what had changed since she had been away. She had, she decided, tired of the tranquil green of the ocean.

The land over which Tessa floated was a dry, unhappy place. There were people always hungry, always dying, always thirsty. It was there, for the first time, that Tessa learned that there were still ways that humans, in all their crafty ingenious ways, could hurt a cloud.

From afar Tessa saw a plane, so puny that if she had had any sort of physical strength she could have crushed it like a bug, fly into a cloud. It disappeared into the white and for a while it was as if it had been swallowed up. And then she saw the cloud begin to rain. Slowly at first and then fiercely and fast. Tessa watched with interest as other little planes pierced the cloud. They moved with purpose and practice and the cloud rained and rained until, slowly, it shrank and shrank into nothing at all. The ground was fed, the sun shone through, and down below Tessa could see the people come out to enjoy the sun and prepare the earth.

From where she was Tessa let loose a small rainfall so that down below, villagers caught outdoors were forced to run and take shelter inside shops and restaurants, complaining loudly all the while about the unseasonable rain which the weather stations had not given sufficient warning for.

From then on Tessa confined herself to cities, major metropolises so vast that it took her days to shift around and where she could count on the presence of other clouds to hide her movements.

It was a lonely existence. Once again she was at the mercy of those who chose to see her, and pictures were taken so freely. But what was worse was that she now noticed more than ever the way the humans bunched together in groups. Schoolgirls grabbing their friends to run hand in hand across streets in defiance of the traffic lights. Grandparents who held the hands of their toddler grandchildren, each generation so weak on their legs that it was impossible to tell who was guiding who. One night a flicker of light on top of a high-rise building caught her eye. Despite the night chill there was a couple who had spread out a blanket on the rooftop. One of them had thought to bring a flashlight and they were tracing shapes into the clouds, carving light into the darkness. It was the man of the couple who seemed the most eager to be there, who kept finding little excuses to reach for and touch the woman who lay by his side.

But she was the one who finally reached for him, turning and taking his face in both her hands and kissing him with a gentleness that would have made Tessa sigh if it had been possible for clouds to sigh. Up there on the rooftop in the cold night air they peeled off just enough of their clothes so that they could couple together and they moved with the shy yet steady embrace of new lovers taking joy in each other's bodies for the first time.

Tessa had not thought of Brick for a long, long time but she thought of him then. Thought of the early days of their courtship when she had been dizzy with her desire. They had spent whole days in bed till the pleasure and the lust had left her spent and shameless, so tired and loved that even the thought of draping a sheet over her body left her feeling exhausted. The only times they bothered to untangle themselves was when their baser instincts drove them to do so. They took to the bathroom and washed their bodies half-heartedly under water so hot it felt more purifying than the soap and shampoo that did the dirty work of keeping them clean. They had reluctantly dried themselves and dressed and then tottered off into the street where they thought they were being so modest by not tearing each other's clothes off but where they were actually making everyone else uncomfortable with their little glances and their caressing hands which wandered longingly over each other's bodies. There was a pizza place around the corner from Tessa's studio apartment and she and Brick used to go there, the only in-store customers. They would eat the greasy food and kiss in-between bites and, when they were especially loving, lick the grease off each other's fingers like animals. Tessa had never felt more sated.

Sometimes, after they were married, when it was her turn to make dinner and she simply could not, she would pick up her phone and order pizza for the girls from that same chain. The girls loved pizza nights, their unpredictability only contributing to their charm. Brick always hated pizza night and complained loudly and Tessa did as well, even though she was always the one who ordered it.

Somehow throughout the decades and through thousands of different managers and a million indifferent teens resentfully working their way through their first part-time jobs, the pizza always tasted exactly the same. Yet eating something when she was loved up and starving and eating something when she had had over a decade to enrich her palate was quite different. Expensive wines, dark chocolate, sharp cheeses, and organic vegetables straight from the farm had spoiled the charms of the pizza. When Tessa ate the pizza there was the experience of eating of it, which sickened her, and then, like an aftertaste, there was the memory of how good she had once considered it. It was hard to reconcile these two things.

And yet now that she was out of her body what Tessa wouldn't have given for a taste of that pizza on her tongue. She remembered what it felt like for the heavy dough to settle thickly in her stomach rendering her inert. If she had been able to eat the pizza now it would have tasted good for she was starving again only this time for the physical.

Tessa remembered being an ugly, unloved teenager lying on her bed, motionless, feeling that if she wasn't touched, and soon, she would simply die. That was the feeling she could remember from her before life that most closely compared to what she felt as a cloud.

She had spent so much time in the before annoyed with her body, disliking her body, wishing she simply didn't have one. But she had not sloughed off her problems when she turned into a cloud, only created new and complicated ones. Her body had been her first and only home. Now she was rendered stateless, incapable of either pain or pleasure.

When they were done with each other the couple on the roof struggled back into their clothes, buttoning up buttons, zipping up zippers, and smoothing out collars. They gave each other long, lingering kisses in-between clothing themselves. They folded up their blanket and made sure they had left nothing behind and then hand in hand they went through a little door that brought them back into the safety and warmth of the building.

Outside a little cloud drifted away.

Tessa let the winds take her far away from human eyes, to reach the uppermost portion of the sky she could tangle with. The cloud cover blocked the earth from her view and she turned her gaze towards the dizzying sky up above and looked out into space, the planets and stars calling to her. And between herself and all that wild unknown she caught a hint of something she had only seen before in fragments, a shimmer, more suggestion than reality. Was it another cloud, drifting where she had never seen a cloud before?

There was only one way to find out and the wind beckoned while the cloud sparkled to her, calling her name.

". . . also known by the common name *rain clouds* which sounds much better than *nimbus*. Why is everything in Latin anyway? Surely there should be a better way, for example, if it were up to me I would stray away from the Latin and perhaps to the more poetic and pleasing-sounding *crying clouds*. But then again *crying* comes to English by way of the French *crier* which itself has etymological roots that originate with the Latin . . ."

—*A Dictionary of Clouds*

The year before she turned 30 Rafaela began to get headaches just before it rained, an ailment she thought afflicted only the old. She never thought to mention them, but one evening, as she and Tasha were meeting in front of the NAC about to hear Dvořák in concert, she winced and held her hand to her forehead.

—What's wrong?

—Oh, nothing. I've started getting these weird headaches. Pressure headaches before the rain starts.

Tasha had looked up at the sky, at the dense uniform clouds hanging low overhead.

—I get those too.

They never discussed their mother anymore except in the vaguest terms. Their grandmother Garnett had been the only one who had talked about it openly, and the older she became the more others took it as a sign of senility, dismissing her the way older women were often dismissed, with a condescending smile. She had died quite suddenly when Rafaela was 24. She had been fine and then a car had hit her, knocking her down and causing her hip to break. The decline was quite rapid after that, only a few months. During that time each day seemed to stretch out interminably long as the uncertainty of knowing whether that day would be the day she died made every second an agony.

The last time the girls saw her she was in the hospital after a routine checkup had led her to be admitted for a several-day stay. She appeared quite cheery and well. She didn't have enough energy to keep her eyes open, but she asked the girls to talk around her and smiled as she listened.

Towards the end of the visit when the girls were getting ready to go she opened her eyes to look at them one last time.

—I know you'll be well, she told them. Don't worry about me. Maybe like your mother I'll turn into a cloud. Wouldn't that be something? Wouldn't that be wonderful?

They never saw her alive again. Each girl privately thought of it less as the moment when they had last seen their grandmother Garnett and more as the last time they heard someone speak of their mother turning into a cloud.

There had also been trouble in the form of their mother's brother, their uncle Casi. He had never believed his sister would leave her girls and eventually the police had been called and had interviewed Brick and both the children who uniformly stuck to the same story. Tessa had been acting strangely for some time. After a family vacation she had disappeared. Tasha was a bad liar and while the police repeatedly pressured her, she reluctantly revealed that she had been the last one to see her mother and that her mother had slipped out in the middle of the night leaving the family for good.

Though the land around the co-worker's cabin was half-heartedly searched, nothing was ever found. Still, there were those who believed that their father was a murderer. It was the reason that Tasha didn't speak to her uncle Casi, who never stopped suspecting that Brick had killed his sister, and Rafaela wouldn't have known him if she met him on the street. For a few years in high school Tasha had been known as the murderer's daughter, but then she left for university and all traces of the old scandal evaporated in the move. It wasn't all bad though, really. For all that there were people who believed in Brick's guilt there were plenty who believed in his innocence. Among his staunchest defenders was his new girlfriend, a woman who devotedly defended Brick in all matters large and small, a woman who moved in with their father and then combed through his house purging it of traces of Tessa year after year until there were no traces left. Her final, greatest triumph was in isolating Brick from his daughters, so that the two heirs to Tessa's lineage no longer went to his house nor talked to him with the exception of Father's Day and Brick's birthday.

Not all rain brought headaches, but after they found out that they both suffered from them Tasha and Rafaela began to call each other when they sensed one coming so that the other sister could throw open her window and look up at the sky.

They spoke only in oblique terms wondering if the headaches were signs and if they were signs whether they were reading them correctly. They wondered if they would know their mother to see her anymore. They wondered openly whether she and her were the correct pronouns as over a decade of social movements had brought new ways of thinking about gender and more precise terminology to the forefront.

One night Rafaela woke from a deep sleep so abruptly that she reached a hand to her chest to rub out the pain before she realized that it was the pain in her head that had awoken her. She reached for the phone tangled up in the sheets beside her and with sleep-heavy half-lidded eyes she called Tasha. It went through to voicemail. Rafaela knew somehow that Tasha was awake and calling her and neither could answer because both were occupied in calling the other.

Abandoning the phone she left her bedroom and walked down the stairs, clutching at the railing as she did. She had lived in apartments for so long that moving about in a house still felt strange and unusual, so much space to adjust to.

She went out the back door to the patio and being outside alone at night even in a house she owned gave her a feeling like she was sneaking around doing something she wasn't supposed to.

The air was thick and heavy and the second she walked outside she heard it, the cracking of thunder like a sheet of metal being shaken right by her ear.

Then it began to rain. The drops were hard as they pelted down, they made her feel every inch of her vulnerable flesh and left her soaking in seconds. Still Rafaela did not turn around to go inside. She put her hands up to the sky to cup the water in her palms and hoped that in her corner of the city Tasha was feeling it too.

She stayed there until the rain stopped, her feet half buried in the backyard mud, the smell of unleashed earth rising up to meet her.

ACKNOWLEDGEMENTS

Thank you to my sister, Tanya, for her genuine and uncomplicated pride every time I tried, even when trying meant failure.

Thank you to my parents, Aris and Trudi, for always believing I could do this.

Some of these stories were previously published in literary magazines. Thank you to the readers and editors of *The Ottawa Arts Review*, *The Threepenny Review*, *PRISM international*, *The Dark*, *subTerrain*, *LatineLit*, *swamp pink*, and *The O. Henry Prize Stories* for supporting my work.

Thank you to the many journals who told me no in a way kind enough to keep me going.

These stories were funded with grants from the Ontario Arts Council recommended by ECW, The Porcupine's Quill, and Wolsak & Wynn, as well as the City of Ottawa's Cultural Fund. Thank you to the people of Ottawa and Ontario for funding these grants.

Thank you to my agent, Ron Eckel, for his calm guidance through the business end of writing.

Thank you to my editor, Jen Albert, who gave me the space to be my best and strangest self.

Thank you to *The Girl Who Cried Diamonds* ECW team for the roles they played bringing my book to production.

Editor: Jen Albert
Editorial manager: Sammy Chin
Sales director: Emily Ferko
Art director: Jessica Albert
Cover designer: Caroline Suzuki
Copy editor: Crissy Calhoun
Proofreader: Jen Knoch
Publicist: Emily Varsava

Early versions of these stories appeared
in the following publications:

"The Girl on the Metro" in *The Ottawa Arts Review*

"A Golden Light" in *The Threepenny Review* and
The O. Henry Prize Winning Stories

"Common Animals" in *PRISM international*

"An Occupation" in *PRISM international*

"Mother" in *The Dark*

"Goodbye, Melody" in *subTerrain*

"The Singing Keys" in *LatineLit*

"Damage Control" in *swamp pink*.